ALSO BY CRISTINA GARCÍA

Novels

A Handbook to Luck
Monkey Hunting
The Agüero Sisters
Dreaming in Cuban

Anthologies

Bordering Fires: The Vintage Book of Contemporary Mexican and Chicano/a Literature

¡Cubanísimo!: The Vintage Book of Contemporary Cuban Literature

Children's Books

I Wanna Be Your Shoebox
The Dog Who Loved the Moon

Poetry

The Lesser Tragedy of Death

The Lady Matador's Hotel

A NOVEL

Cristina García

Scribner

NEW YORK LONDON TORONTO SYDNEY

Scribner
A Division of Simon & Schuster, Inc.
1230 Avenue of the Americas
New York, NY 10020

First Scribner hardcover edition September 2010

SCRIBNER and design are registered trademarks of The Gale Group,
Inc., used under license by Simon & Schuster, Inc., the publisher
of this work.

For information about special discounts for bulk purchases,
please contact Simon & Schuster Special Sales at 1-866-506-1949
or business@simonandschuster.com.

The Simon & Schuster Speakers Bureau can bring authors to your
live event. For more information or to book an event contact the
Simon & Schuster Speakers Bureau at 1-866-248-3049 or
visit our website at www.simonspeakers.com.

Book design by Ellen R. Sasahara

Manufactured in the United States of America

1 3 5 7 9 10 8 6 4 2

Library of Congress Control Number: 2009049749

ISBN 978-1-4391-8174-4
ISBN 978-1-4391-8176-8 (ebook)

For Lol and Camille

Their incandescent reliefs, their passages, they are a mournful, single-chorded psalm . . .

—Coral Bracho

The Lady Matador's Hotel

CHAPTER ONE

The lady matador puts on her suit of lights •
The ex-guerrilla serves pork chops • The lawyer delivers a
baby girl • The Korean manufacturer visits his mistress •
The poet buys a cheap wristwatch • In the gym with
the colonel • The news

SUNDAY

But I have in me all the dreams of the world.

    —Fernando Pessoa

Room 719

The lady matador stands naked before the armoire mirror and unrolls her long pink stockings. She likes to put these on first, before the fitted pants and the stark white shirt, before the bullioned waistcoat and the ribs-length jacket densely embroidered with sequins and beads; before the braces, and the soft black slippers, and the wisp of silk at her throat; before the *montera,* an authentic one she ordered from a bullfighters' shop in Madrid, which sits atop her hair, pulled back in a single braid; before her cape, voluminous as a colony of bats.

Suki Palacios has come a long way to this spired hotel in the tropics, to this wedge of forgotten land between continents, to this place of hurricanes and violence and calculated erasures. She arrived yesterday from Los Angeles, trading the moody squalor of one city for another, the broken Spanish for one more lyrical. In a week she will compete in the first Battle of the Lady Matadors in the Americas. Suki is here early to display her skills and generate enthusiasm for the fight. By the time the other *matadoras* arrive in the capital, its citizens will be clamoring for blood.

Every window of the hotel looks inward to a crosshatch of courtyards and fountains, banyans and Madeira palms. The pool is visible beneath Suki's window, a glazed and artificial blue. A cascade of bougainvillea brightens the patio. Aviaries with raucous jungle parrots outmatch the mariachis in volume and plumage. The lady matador is tempted to submit to the hotel's shielding niceties, to ignore the afternoon torpor awaiting her in the ring. She's grown accustomed to the jeering spectators who come to spit at her and provoke the bulls. They would gladly banish her from the sport altogether—interloper, scandalous woman playing at being a man.

Suki will ignore them. She'll keep a watchful eye on each bull, on the thick hump of its beckoning neck muscle, which, if pierced properly, will lead her straight to its heart. Before the final thrust of her sword will come preludes of ritual and fear: the whip of her red muleta; the stink of the bristling bull as it passes; her pivoting hips as she winds the beast around her in dizzying succession; the reverse slide across the dusty ring, fluttering her cape like butterfly wings. And always, the clamorous heat. As she awaits the bull's last charge, sword in hand, in the *suerte de recibir,* her mouth will flood with a mineral saltiness, as if some essential earthly cycle has been fulfilled.

The lady matador devours the sliced pear she ordered, at great expense, from room service. The pear is unsatisfactory, hard and mealy, but she finishes it, seeds and all. Later there will be time for more agreeable, local fruit. Last night Suki visited the cathedral, off the colonial plaza. It was All Souls Day and the whisperings to the dead rose from the pews, circling in the naves until they hummed with a humid sorrow. Suki trusts in the enigmas of the unknown as she does her own eyesight, or the pumping muscles of her heart. The trick is balancing the measurable known against the vast chaos that defines everything else. In medical school, Suki's professors praised her for her lack of sentimentality but they underestimated her respect for the imperceptible.

In the cathedral, Suki slipped a fifty-dollar bill into the offerings box and carefully lit fourteen candles, one for every year she and her mother were both alive. Ritual is everything. Her father, a professional dancer, taught her this. Fourteen candles for her dead mother. Pink stockings first. One sliced ripe pear. For extra luck, silent sex with a stranger two days before a fight. (On Friday, she'd found a suitable partner at an Hermosa Beach discotheque.) Then in the shadowed moment before she steps into the ring, Suki repeats three words in Spanish and Japanese: *arrogance, honor, death.*

The lady matador checks her profile in the dresser mirror, the profile her father insists is her grandfather's, a redheaded Mexican bullfighter who was famous in the thirties. Ramón Palacios lasted one season in Spain—billed as El Azteca, he fought in the same rings as the legendary Manolete and Joselito—before a severe goring forced him back to Veracruz with a lame left leg. Suki's father grew up listening to Abuelo Ramón's stories along with the instantaneous revisions by his wife, an upper-class *sevillana* he'd seduced at the height of his success. Abuelo Ramón was fond of saying that only matadors, like angels, can tame death and become immortal.

Suki fastens her cape and, with a final look around her, sweeps out of the room. She passes a cluster of military men in the hallway, formal in their decorated khaki uniforms. From their uptight demeanor, Suki guesses they're from Chile. The officers are too dazzled by her to speak; fearful, perhaps, that the lady matador might turn out to be a disturbingly beautiful man.

The elevator doors open to reveal a row of Latin American generals. Suki fights the urge to inspect their medals, pluck a few shiny ones for herself. Instead she nods briskly and joins them. Conversation stops as the men pause to inhale the lady matador's alluring scent of pear and French perfume.

"You will fight the bulls today?" The voice comes from the back of the descending elevator in confident, accented English. It belongs to a droopy-eyed colonel, broad across the chest.

"*Sí,*" Suki answers languidly as the elevator doors open. Then she strides across the bustling lobby of the hotel, where a bellboy whistles for the limousine that will take her to the ring.

Garden Restaurant

Dozens of military men from around the Americas, old fraternities of criminals, are making the ex-guerrilla nervous. Today they are her customers, gathered in groups of seven or eight, fussing over their fried pork chops and eggs. It astounds her that these men can sit around like princes without fear or restraints. Aura Estrada wills her hands to stop trembling as she serves them. As she tries to ignore their conversations—about subversives, whorehouses, hidden encampments in the sierra—what she wants more than anything is to be invisible. Barring that, she'd just as soon cut their throats.

The ex-guerrilla crosses herself, trying to tamp down her fury as she waits for more pork chops from the chef. One of the generals sent his back, complaining that they were too tough. *"A sus órdenes,"* Aura said, taking his plate. She noticed him noticing her as she walked away.

When the pork chops are ready Aura discreetly spits on them, working in the saliva until they gleam. Once she'd laid booby traps against scum like him, fired machine guns, threw grenades at passing army trucks. So this is what she's been reduced to? Rubbing a gob of spit on some killer's pork chops?

Her sisters, both nuns, take turns writing to Aura in their florid convent penmanship, ungrammatical sentences that look like inky balustrades across the onionskin sheets. *God will punish the barbarians,* promises the fat-cheeked Cristina, *if not in this life then the next you must believe this or perish in doubt may the Lord bless you dearest Sister.* Telma, eleven months younger and grown plump from inaction, is more succinct: *Pray to Saint Anthony.*

Aura rarely prays but when she does it's to her beloved dead: to Papi, who passed away when she was ten of a blood disease that the curanderas couldn't heal; to her brother, Julio, set aflame by a sadistic army patrol while defending the family's cornfield; to Mamá, who, after helplessly witnessing her only son's death, stopped eating and sleeping until her soul joined his; to Aura's lover, Juan Carlos, blown apart by a land mine.

If she begins to tally the savagery, she wouldn't stop. Tío Luís, jeep-dragged up the mountainside to a bloody pulp. Cousin Belinda, killed by a rifle shoved between her thighs. Padre Josué's head impaled on a stick and left at the chapel door. This was during the first summer's violence, when the nights suffocated. Tito, the shy, long-lashed boy whom Aura liked: gone. Yes, there were coffins, pine-wood coffins stacked up to the sky. The civil war might've ended years ago but the grief, the grief is flourishing still.

The ex-guerrilla smoothes her pink-and-white apron and brings the general his pork chops on a round metal tray. If only the tray were a discus with deadly serrated edges, like the ones in kung fu movies. With a flash of her wrist she could decapitate the general on the spot. But no good would come of this. One butcher dead for countless poor souls. *Que Dios me ayude,* Aura silently prays. She must stop these hallucinations or risk going insane. Aura sets the pork chops before the general, who pats his stomach with both hands.

"Now they look extra juicy," he says, giving her a wink.

"*¿Algo más, General?*"

"Save me some of your most delicious dessert." The snub-nosed general says this loud enough for the neighboring tables to hear. Everyone brays on cue.

Men are so ridiculous, Aura thinks, bowing curtly; and because they fear ridicule, they're exceedingly dangerous. She's seen this for herself time and again: a man would sooner kill another than suffer the slightest embarrassment.

Aura attends to her other customers. Senator Silvestre Jiménez and his girlfriend are at their usual table, signaling for more mimosas. The two are here to gauge their social standing, which has plummeted since the senator left his wife. In the capital, nobody looks askance at a man who keeps a mistress but it is indecent and unmanly to abandon the mother of one's children, then make a public spectacle of her replacement.

The president of the Universal Fruit Company, Federico Ladrón-Benes, is enjoying his *cafecito* near the bougainvillea, his face buried in the day's headlines. During her break, Aura will read his discarded newspaper. She's following the election news with great interest. It's unthinkable to her that the ex-dictator is running for president—and with an astonishing amount of support from the very people he brutalized. This time he's claiming to be a born-again Christian. His slogan—ON A MISSION FROM GOD—is plastered everywhere in the capital. If he wins, she'll have to find a way to leave the country for good.

Aura surveys her section of the restaurant, which is part indoors, part out. The latest addition to the garden is a pair of skittish peacocks. Their shrieks send chills up her neck. They, too, will prove as transient as the wealthy guests. The landscaping was designed to resemble the jungles Aura lived in for months. In those days she'd carried a hunter's knife and, for a time, a Russian pistol. No one at the restaurant has any idea about her previous life. What they do know is that she suffered in the war; in that she's no different from anyone else.

Aura is convinced that the entire country has succumbed to a collective amnesia. This is what happens in a society where no one is permitted to grow old slowly. Nobody talks of the past, for fear their wounds might reopen. Privately, though, their wounds never heal.

The parrots chatter shrilly in their aviaries, screeching invective and snatches of poetry. The bartender, with great patience, has taught the ornately crested one to say *No me dicen que hay patria pequeña*—there's no such thing as a small country—to the amusement of the Miraflor's privileged guests. Aura wonders how many of these guests know that the line is from a poem by a famous Nicaraguan revolutionary who would've detested the likes of them. *A great flock of crows is staining the sky.* This, too, is one of the poet's lines and it happens to be true just now.

A starched-looking colonel settles down at the last empty table with an entourage of foreign officers. They wear identical sunglasses, wraparound and impenetrable. Except for the colonel, who has a tiny rearview mirror clipped to his left lens. Aura tries to figure out where the men are from: Argentina? Paraguay? Peru? An oversized American sits to the colonel's right. What offenses will they be plotting next against *el pueblo*? The ex-guerrilla approaches their table with eight menus. The busboy distributes water, napkins, silverware, removes the urn of flowers at the colonel's request.

The colonel resembles a lot of military men in her country, high-cheeked and chisel-jawed, though exceptionally thick through the chest. His arm muscles bulge grotesquely from his sleeves. Only the faint rash on his neck mutes the menacing effect. Another U.S.-trained puppet, no doubt. The gringos are in full force at the military conference this week. They've never claimed to be more than advisers but everyone knows what they "advise": killing leftists, securing black market weapons, staging well-timed coups. The civil war couldn't have lasted as long as it did without them. Aura spies the Americans at the hotel gym, lifting enormous barbells, groaning loud enough for everyone to take notice. Most of them look too inflexible to tie their shoes.

"Something to drink, gentlemen?"

The American orders a Bloody Mary and everyone follows

suit. It's no wonder these officers commit the atrocities they do. Not a single one has a mind of his own. Aura places their order. The bartender, Miguel, raises his eyebrows then shrugs noncommittally. Yesterday he boasted of dropping a measure of stool hardener in the Americans' drinks. Aura laughed to imagine the *yanquis,* red-faced, trying to shit bricks.

The bartender shares Aura's love for Bruce Lee movies, and for the same reason as she: the forces of evil don't stand a chance against him. Most nights, Aura falls asleep watching *Fist of Fury,* or *Enter the Dragon,* over a late-night dinner of hotel leftovers. She rents a room less than a mile away with a hot plate and a communal shower. Now and then she splurges on Chinese takeout, usually fried rice or spicy noodles with beef. Aura read an interview with Lee once in which he said, "Fighting is not something sought after, yet it is something that seeks you."

At the colonel's table everyone orders pork chops, again following the American's lead. Aura recalls her guerrilla-training pamphlets, the ones printed in Havana, exhorting her to take the revolution into her own hands. *The struggle is your personal burden.* Years ago she'd desperately wanted to visit Cuba. Her lover, Juan Carlos, had trained there for ten months. He told her that Cubans lived decently. Nobody was starving. Children didn't die of simple things like diarrhea. Every citizen could read and write.

In the kitchen, the chef is screaming over a crab enchilada scorched to leather by his clumsy assistant. Aura puts in her order for more pork chops. "Is this a fucking national holiday for pork chops, *¿qué?*" The chef glares at her, his toque perilously askew. Aura ignores him and rubs her left leg, newly overrun with a varicose vein. Then she returns to her customers. A couple she hasn't seen before is sitting at a table for two; Americans, judging by their clothes. No one else would be caught dead dressing so shabbily for Sunday brunch. The woman wrinkles her nose and orders the assorted pastry plate, as if disapproving of her choice in advance. The husband wants the damn pork chops and a basket of tortillas.

"*A sus órdenes,*" Aura says, forcing a smile, and pours them their first cups of coffee.

The Lobby

The lawyer stares out the tinted window of her chauffeured Mercedes as it maneuvers through the streets of the capital. Political posters are everywhere, a strident backdrop to marketplace vendors hawking breadfruit, brooms, balloons. The presidential elections are less than a week away and run-down electioneering cars clog the already hopeless traffic. Skinny men shout from rolled-down windows, megaphones in hand, or through crackling speakers perched on their roofs.

Gertrudis Stüber knows personally each of the eleven candidates running for president and every congressional aspirant besides. She makes it her business to know them. Only the leftists resist her offers. For this reason, and for their enduring political bilge, the lawyer despises them. Gertrudis was seduced by their lies decades ago, specifically by one bearded revolutionary with whom she fell abjectly, embarrassingly, in love. Of course, this was before law school and marriage and the reality of the courts and corruptible judges.

Her secretary, Elva Flores, holds a sleeping baby girl beside her in the backseat of the sedan. Gertrudis turns to inspect the child before they arrive at the Hotel Miraflor. The girl is pretty enough, with straight hair and an acceptable nose. She's wrapped in a cotton blanket patterned with flying elephants. The lawyer buys the blankets in bulk, along with dressy baby clothes, from a Korean textiles manufacturer on the outskirts of town. She requires her wards to meet their parents in the same standard outfit. There is a romance to the business of babies and the lawyer wants to ensure that love occurs at first sight.

"What's her name?" Gertrudis asks.

"It's not settled yet." Elva hands her boss the child's adoption folder. "The birth mother put Concha on the birth certificate but the caretaker has been calling her Esperanza and the adoptive parents are debating between Beatriz and Monique."

"That's more than I need to know."

"I'm sorry, Doctora."

"And her health?"

"Just a recurring vaginal infection but otherwise normal."

"Is she clear for today?"

"Yes." The secretary twists a corner of the baby blanket between her thumb and forefinger. After two years of working for the lawyer, Elva is as flustered as she was on her first day. She wants to dislike *la doctora,* but it isn't so easy. Her boss is smart and capable, and she expects Elva to be the same. It's this straightforwardness that Elva most appreciates. Plus *la doctora* is very generous at Christmastime. The truth is, Elva loves the babies no matter how cynically they're conceived.

As the chauffeur pulls the sedan into the hotel's colonnaded entrance, the lawyer catches a glimpse of the lady matador, blinding in a gold suit of lights, stepping into a limousine.

"Now I've seen it all," the chauffeur says. "A woman fighting bulls! What do they want to do next? Fly to the moon?"

"In fact, women astronauts have already circled the earth," Gertrudis retorts icily.

"That was a woman?" Elva blurts out.

"*Sí, señorita,*" the chauffeur continues, his dentures clacking. "Didn't you read today's paper? She's from Los Angeles, part Mexican, part *chinita*. You know how those Americans mix up everything."

"That's enough, Armando. Now park over here. We'll be back in ten minutes."

A hotel doorman opens the car door. The crowd parts for Gertrudis as she glides through the lobby, resplendent with chandeliers. She's six feet tall in low-heeled pumps and her fuchsia Italian suit sets off her fair complexion. Only descending the grand staircase would make a more impressive entrance. Those who don't know Gertrudis Stüber speculate about her identity. Those who do, nod in her direction. She isn't one to be crossed in the back rooms of the country's tractable legal system. The worst charge against her? That she thinks and acts like a man. To Gertrudis, this is the ultimate compliment. Only her husband, a distant German cousin with effeminate manners, softens her impression.

Gertrudis isn't maternally inclined. She inherited this from her own mother, who, when pregnant with Gertrudis, rode horses from morning to dusk. In her sixth month, the doctor ordered Mutti to bed on account of a partially dislodged cervical plug, a result, they said, of her vigorous schedule. Bedridden and restless, her mother soon began reading as voraciously as she rode. She grew obsessed with Thomas Mann's *Magic Mountain* and read it nine times, always hoping for a different ending.

The lawyer spots her clients at the far end of the lobby, where a diminutive violinist serenades hotel guests with a Dvorak sonata. Gertrudis sizes up the couple in an instant. It's obvious that the wife is the one driving the adoption. Every one of their checks has been drawn on her account. The husband looks reluctant but pliable behind his graying goatee. He has the lazy gestures of a man who lives in his head.

The costs of operating what Gertrudis privately calls her "export" business are mounting. There are the breeder mothers to take care of (her biggest expense at a thousand dollars per pregnancy). The stud services of a few select men. The fees of the increasingly finicky caretaker families. Supplies of baby formula, clothes, and disposable diapers (nobody wants to wash cloth ones anymore). Medical and hospital expenses. A phalanx of judges and politicians paid to look the other way. The lobbyists' ever-swelling salaries. The upkeep of her fancy offices downtown. A percentage to her co-agents in the United States. Skyrocketing website and Internet advertising costs.

Her price for a healthy newborn: thirty thousand U.S. dollars.

On the plus side are the kickbacks Gertrudis gets from requiring her clients to stay at the most expensive hotel in the capital. Her arrangement with the Miraflor's general director is mutually lucrative. Last year, Gertrudis pushed through seventeen adoptions in spite of myriad legal and legislative obstacles and a spate of bad press. This year she's managed to complete only fourteen but seven more are in the pipeline. She plans to rush these through before Christmas. The holidays are high season for adopting babies.

Elva struggles to keep up with her long-legged boss. The flying-elephants blanket billows as she runs. She carries the baby girl, who stirs and blinks in confusion before drifting back to sleep. Elva adjusts her glasses and stretches out her hand to the waiting parents. "It's a pleasure to meet you," she stammers. "This is Doctora Stüber, your lawyer. She is the, eh, angel who makes all of this possible." Elva was instructed to memorize this introduction from the beginning. She's uttered it dozens of times but it catches in her throat just the same.

Gertrudis takes the baby from Elva and settles it on her hip while she reviews the rules of their visit: no leaving the hotel with the baby; meals must be eaten at the hotel; formula and baby supplies must be purchased at the hotel sundries shop; contacting the birth mother or caretaker family is strictly prohibited; no petitioning for the baby's custody at any government office except as designated by the lawyer herself; no guarantees that the baby will be permanently released to them during this trip; no refunds issued on any portion of their deposits; no assumption of liability in case of accident or death while the child is in their custody.

"Is that clear?" Gertrudis makes it sound more like a command than a question. Her secretary holds out the paperwork for the adoptive parents to sign. They look uncomfortable but agree to the terms. (They always agree to the terms.) Only after they both sign does the lawyer surrender the squirming infant.

"My sincere best wishes to you both," Gertrudis says before turning to carve a straight path through the lobby, clotted with high-ranking military officers from around the Americas. The last thing the lawyer hears as she slips into the revolving brass doors is the wail of the baby girl she's just deposited with her new parents.

Honeymoon Suite

Won Kim bends toward his mistress and breathes in the milky fragrance of her neck. Asleep in the darkened hotel suite, her face appears gentle and moonlike, nothing like it does when she is awake. Awake, the same face is all moving angles, incongruous, impossible to predict. Anyone happening upon his mistress might mistake her for a young girl napping, except for the fact of her belly, eight months pregnant with his child.

The television is on, flickering in its faux antique cabinet. The reporter interviews a lady matador who will be giving a bullfighting demonstration this afternoon. The woman is originally from California but speaks an easy Spanish. She says: "A glorious death is what everyone craves."

A shred of torn wallpaper catches Won Kim's eye. It reminds him of a dying moth. He has been thinking a lot about death lately, though he is only thirty-nine and reasonably healthy. Won Kim lights a cigarette and eyes the French doors to the balcony, wondering if it is high enough to plunge off successfully. A strip of clouds looks like a string of pearls in the sky. Sparrows chatter in the banyan trees, taunting him to fly. A headache slowly builds in his temples.

Won Kim drifts toward the bathroom of the honeymoon suite in search of aspirin and a washcloth. He is tempted to fill the tub with scalding water, ease himself in, and drop in a live appliance; the hair dryer perhaps, or his electric shaver from Hong Kong. He takes a deep breath and waits for his desperation to subside. He knows what his father would have called him: a coward, too soft in the flesh. What Won Kim longs for most is to return to the butterfly reserve in the highlands, with its soothing laboratories of chrysalis and pupa. He needs a period of dormancy, a chance to recollect himself before tackling the complexities of his life.

Fact: His mistress, Berta Acosta, is fifteen years old—sixteen next Friday—and her family knows nothing of her pregnancy. (Won Kim half expects a brother or uncle of hers to come after him with a machete.)

Fact: His textiles factory has been hemorrhaging money for two years. (Competition from China and the worsening economy are to blame.)

Fact: His mother is dying and has beseeched him, a bachelor, for: (a) a grandson (his two older sisters have produced only girls); (b) to return home to Seoul; and (c) to bury her with fanfare in the old tradition.

Fact: Since Won Kim learned that his mistress was pregnant, he can no longer make love to her, or to anyone else. (Until Berta, he'd had sex only with prostitutes. Now even this is impossible; confirmed twice, with great humiliation, at a reputable brothel.)

Fact: Won Kim's doctor says that if he does not quit smoking, he will surely have a heart attack. (His chest pains have grown more severe of late.)

Won Kim inspects the honeymoon suite. His mistress has taken needle and thread to the hotel's pillows, which she has stitched with howler monkeys. Berta is a talented embroiderer; this was her job at the textiles factory, after all. Unfortunately, her fancy handiwork here will cost him a fortune. Berta has recounted to him almost nothing of her life before she sought work in the capital. The truth is, Won Kim does not want to learn much about her. He is not proud of this.

A porcelain cup on the nightstand looks to him like a

minuscule skull. The remains of his mistress's orange soda fizzes there. Just as Won Kim is thinking the porcelain cup could be his own fragile skull, Berta wakes up and flings the cup across the room, smashing it to pieces.

"What the hell?" he sputters.

"Scars in the heavens," she hisses with cracked lips.

Won Kim hates when his mistress speaks to him in riddles, something she started in her fifth month of pregnancy, about the time she began eating six poached eggs a day, the yolks soft, nearly raw. Every week brings a rash of surprises, as if the baby inside her were issuing directives designed expressly to disturb his peace of mind. Berta has thrown soap off the balcony, taped hotel stationery to the pink toilet seat. He cannot guess what might be next. If he strung together her nonsensical utterances, Won Kim wonders, would they constitute a manifesto of sorts? A blueprint for his redemption?

As a boy, the closest thing he'd found to transcendence was catching butterflies. But his father discouraged this pursuit, even after he won a nationwide high school competition for most varied species collected. Instead of studying lepidoptery, Won Kim was forced to attend business college in Seoul. He dropped out after a year, worked odd jobs, embarrassing his parents, and traveled to Thailand.

Broke and defeated, he finally accepted a job at his father's firm and was promptly sent to the tropics to run his factory there. It seemed to Won Kim like a promising adventure at the time. That was twelve long years ago. His father's first name, Bon-hwa, means "glorious" and is emblazoned everywhere, most prominently at the factory entrance: GLORIOUS TEXTILES UNLIMITED.

"Would it please you to go downstairs and get something to

eat?" Won Kim offers. It is Sunday and the hotel has put out its most sumptuous buffet.

To his surprise, Berta does not fight him and gets dressed. Or rather, she undresses, then picks her way toward the armoire like she is crossing a minefield. Won Kim considers her young body, swollen with life. Her limbs are short and muscled, her thighs becomingly flared. Her breasts have doubled in size these last months, the nipples darkening to a rich brown. The same rich brown color forms a line that climbs the center of her bulging stomach, mirroring the curve of her buttocks.

Berta was a virgin the one time they made love. Won Kim remembers every touch and scent and sigh of that night. It was like opening a velvet box from which a butterfly flew out, delicate and iridescent. And he was happy, perhaps for the last time. This was the trouble he brought on himself for insisting on unkissed lips.

His mistress puts on a handwoven skirt, typical of her village, and a *huipil* she embroidered herself with double-headed birds. After her outburst with the porcelain cup, she is cooperative and subdued. Not once during her pregnancy has she demanded so much as a *quetzal*. Not once has she ever asked Won Kim to marry her. Neither of them speaks of the future but he is plagued by its uncertainties.

If she gives birth to a girl, Won Kim would be inclined to abandon mother and child. He could purchase a little house for them, set Berta up with a fine loom and a year's supply of cotton wool. If their loneliness were a shop, he would close it down for good. But if Berta gives birth to a son, he would feel obligated to take him to Korea, arrange to have him raised as his own. If the boy resembled him, all the better; his origins would not matter.

If he did not, life would be more difficult. In the end, his family would accept the child. A boy, *his* boy, after a generation of girls. What choice would they have?

There was a big celebration when Won Kim was born in Seoul nearly four decades ago. No matter that his mother had been depressed when she had carried him in her belly. She was dismissed as overly sensitive, a bad match for her brusque husband. For the last two months of her pregnancy, Won Kim's mother visited the zoo daily, urging the puzzled keepers to set the forlorn elephants free. For this reason, Won Kim is convinced, he was born feeling entrapped.

"You look pretty today," Won Kim tells his mistress, and he means it. He holds out his arm for her to take.

Berta does not acknowledge the compliment but links her arm in his just the same.

"They have waffles today." Won Kim wants to order some with maple syrup and sliced strawberries on the side. He likes American-style breakfasts: pancakes and bacon, mounds of scrambled eggs and toast, washed down with volumes of orange juice and coffee.

In the hallway, he and his mistress pass a tourist couple with a whimpering brown infant—Americans who most likely have purchased the child here. There are dozens of them in the hotel these days, speaking loudly from Spanish phrase books, scooping up the country's children like so many souvenirs. The mother stares at the enormity of Berta's belly, then back down at her baby.

"Buena suerte," the father calls out to Won Kim in perfect Spanish. This surprises him but he nods curtly and returns the wish: *"A ustedes también."*

Room 917

The Moráns argued continuously during their plane ride down to the tropics, weighing the merits of one baby name over another. Taking off from New York City, Ricardo Morán wanted to call their new daughter Beatrice, in honor of Dante's elusive love. Over the eastern seaboard of the United States, his wife lobbied for Monique, the name of a great-aunt who'd left her a sketch by Matisse. By the time they flew over the Straits of Florida, they'd temporarily agreed on Eugenia, after his mother in Cuba, who'd died of complications from diabetes at fifty-six. As the plane circled the tropical capital with its stunning blue-black volcanoes, they decided, finally, on Isabel.

Isabel is with them now in their hotel room, fretful and perplexed. Her whimpering turns into a sustained blast of crying that disarms them both. Sarah Morán has only limited experience with children, two nephews to be specific, adolescent sons of her older sister, a divorce lawyer. To his great regret, Ricardo has no experience with children whatsoever, having left Cuba during the Mariel exodus against the wishes of his pregnant ex-wife, who cursed him to the sharks. He's never met his daughter Barbarita, who, he imagines, longs for him as desperately as he longs for her.

"What do we do now?" Sarah shouts above the baby's squalls. As a pastry chef in New York, disaster for her is a fallen soufflé, a shortage of Belgian chocolate, an electric mixer on the fritz. She's capable of fixing these with her culinary tricks—but a screaming child?

"Check her diapers," Ricardo says and turns on the tub's hot faucet.

"What the hell are you doing?"

"Running a bath. I'll take the baby in with me."

"What's wrong with you? I think she's hungry."

"*Mi amor,* you believe everything can be resolved with a truffle."

"Jesus Christ! Get her some milk!"

"Okay, okay." Ricardo fishes around in their carry-on bag for a can of formula, straining to read the microscopic instructions on the back.

"Hurry!"

"*Coño carajo,*" he mutters, spilling the foul-smelling mixture in the bathroom sink. He survived the misery of Cuba, the nearly deadly exodus to Florida, the festering loneliness of exile in New York—and for what? To take orders from his wife like a lowly kitchen slave? There's nothing gentle or merciful about domesticity, that's for damn sure.

His wife has done nothing but complain since she set foot in the tropics. The pastries at brunch nearly sent her over the edge. They were made with lard, she fumed, and barely suitable for doorstops. Naturally, Ricardo wolfed them down along with everything else on his plate, including a pair of gristly pork chops.

"Are you done yet? I could've made tiramisu by now!"

Ricardo appears with a slippery bottle of lumpy, frothy formula. It'll be a miracle, he thinks, if the child survives her first sip. He remembers the stories his mother told about her own pregnancy, how she'd developed excessive cravings for breadfruit, *palomilla* steak, chow mein. When Ricardo was growing up, Mami seemed to him a bundle of continuous want. Her longings grew more varied and virulent with each passing year: raw pig meat, Hawaiian pineapples (infeasible to procure in revolutionary Cuba), chewing tobacco, cockscomb stew.

"Hold on to her a minute." Sarah thrusts the baby at him and grabs the bottle, pinching the nipple and shaking it until the lumps dissolve.

Ricardo settles with Isabel into a plush armchair and turns on the television. It feels good to hold her, to smell her sour skin. There's a feature on a female toreador, a Californian of Mexican and Japanese descent. Recent footage shows her slaying a bull in Tijuana, then promenading around the ring, holding aloft its testicles.

Isabel drinks half the bottle of formula and falls asleep against Ricardo's chest, her legs dangling against his belly. Tranquility spreads through his torso in the exact shape of her slumbering body. So this is what he missed leaving his daughter behind in Cuba. Isabel's pixie feet fit in the palm of one hand. They remind Ricardo of photographs of Chinese women's bound "lotuses," except Isabel's are freshly pink. He wants to mention this to his wife but thinks better of it. If it can't be measured, kneaded, or put in the oven, she isn't interested.

"She'll starve to death." Sarah tries to force the rubber nipple between the baby's lips.

"Just let her rest." Ricardo is pleased to have the upper hand for once. "Why don't you take a nap, too?"

"Don't tell me what to do," Sarah snaps, closely examining the baby's features. "She's pretty cute, don't you think? Yes you are, Isabel. You're a beauty."

Ricardo flips the channels in search of election news. He suspects that the Cubans are behind the leftists' recent surge in the polls. El Comandante knows how to play the region for sympathy. That was how he masterminded the debacle in Nicaragua.

Ricardo tries to calm the growing storm in his chest. He doesn't want to agitate the baby by thinking of politics.

A breathy sigh from Isabel tickles his neck. He looks down at the damp swirl of his daughter's hair. Her head is still warm from her protests. Ricardo has an urge to sprinkle her with violet water, the way his mother used to do after his evening bath. Instead he holds her close and feels her heart, hot in its little rib cage.

The poet steps into the late afternoon heat of the capital. It's a relief to escape his wife's oppressive hovering. The air is congested with exhaust fumes and the stench of days-old garbage. He takes a handkerchief from his pocket and covers his mouth, to filter out impurities. As a child, he suffered from asthma and the thought of asphyxiation still terrifies him. A line of squat women saunters by with baskets of bundled herbs on their heads. He whiffs the air. Only the mint smells familiar but he wants to believe the rest of those herbs could soothe him.

Ricardo finds a quiet café on the plaza and settles down with a stack of magazines and an espresso. He's eager to soak in the scene, write some poetry. A plate of fried plantains wouldn't hurt, either, but he doubts they're available here. To spend his days reading and writing in a sidewalk café would suit him perfectly. Observation, Ricardo thinks, is the only defensible use of one's time.

The trees grow luminously hazel as the afternoon fades. Mourning doves coo in the lowest branches. Swallows swoop like wayward arrows from one destination to the next. Every living thing is under dusk's spell. Across the plaza, vendors are hustling to earn their last coins for the day. The coconut vendor is particularly vociferous, juggling his wares to get attention. Ricardo is half tempted to call over the boy with watches for sale and tell him there's no point in hawking his timepieces. If the earth's entire existence could be compressed into a day, humans would show up in the last minute and seventeen seconds.

The poet flips through several magazines, checking his horoscope, but there's nothing exciting in store for Capricorns today. Ricardo is impressed with the variety of local offerings. One periodical is dedicated to nothing but photographs of grisly bus accidents. Another sports thick-thighed women in bikinis lewdly riding motorcycles. The glossiest of the publications features that lady matador from TV on the cover, looking sleek as an eel. Her name is Suki Palacios and the article says she's staying at the Hotel Miraflor for a week.

We are the news / We are the light, the poet scribbles in his pocket notebook, then crosses it out. It sounds like a bad political slogan, something El Comandante might have dreamed up. Ricardo detested the Cuban revolution's distortions, the magnetism of its crass, one-size-fits-all propaganda. During his last year in Havana, everyone communicated through subtext and his friends resorted to writing science fiction to fool the censors. He could spend the rest of his days cataloging the ruins.

"Swiss watch, mister?" It's the vendor Ricardo spotted earlier. He's holding up a wristwatch inlaid with fake mother-of-pearl. The poet considers the boy's face, smooth except for the stubble edging his chin.

"More here. Look!" His garish display is clipped to a canvas belt—purple watches with polka dots, a rainbow one with a gyrating smiley face.

"*¿Cuánto por el azúl?*" Ricardo asks, catching him off guard.

"Twenty dollars," the boy persists in English, as if the poet's Spanish came well rehearsed from a phrase book. "Very cheap."

"For everything?" Ricardo decides to play the game.

"Okay, okay, ten dollars."

It's still too much but Ricardo buys it anyway, as a souvenir and a gesture toward fate. He's here to begin over, to become the father he couldn't be nearly a quarter century ago. Time starts now, he thinks, handing over the money. "Are you a Communist?"

The boy backs away. "I sell watches, mister. That's all, I swear."

Ricardo is sorry to have scared the vendor. He wants to say that democracy's net rarely drops down far enough to help the poor but Communism is no solution.

On the far side of the plaza, a barefoot young woman trudges across the cobblestones with a bucket of what looks like red paint, leaving a trail of footprints. A few people straggle in her wake. The poet peels off the plastic coating on the face of his new watch and sets the time to the nearby clock tower. As he's winding it, the screw comes off, freezing the hour forever at twelve minutes after six.

Gym

Colonel Martín Abel is working out at the hotel gym. He's bench-pressing 220 pounds, 80 percent of his body weight, a high portion of it hard muscle. By his fourth set, the barbell will weigh 350 pounds. The colonel enjoys the satisfying clank of the weights, the strain in his chest from exerting himself to maximum capacity. He revels in the girth of his biceps, his sculpted pectorals, the steel-tight compartments of his abdomen. Everywhere he trained in the United States, the Americans referred to stomachs like his as "six-packs."

It was a coup for him to help organize this year's hemispheric military conference in the capital. Top officials from twenty-two nations have come to compare notes on defeating insurgents, asserting their political relevance, swapping the latest torture and detainment techniques. Together these men are responsible for preventing the leftists from gaining ground in Latin America. In times like these, the military needs to stick together. Reaffirm its mission. The colonel knows firsthand the rituals and camaraderie of army life. How soldiers must live wholly in their bodies yet remain professionally detached from the suffering of others. How it's more palatable to battle *enemy, guerrilla, Communist* than *mother, sister, son.*

Martín likes to think he keeps a machine gun embedded between his eyes, the clarity of built-in crosshairs. This is what distinguishes him from the politicians and the five-star generals with their fat offshore bank accounts and weapons contracts. He's tired of their worn-out speeches, of their parades and flash-frozen photographs, of their need to be envied, admired, feared. Not a single one of them appreciates the subtle arts of persuasion, the importance of permanent conversions. This is the colonel's specialty: sucking out the doubting spaces in the brain.

From the gym's sliding glass doors, Martín can see the pool and hotel gardens. The leaves of the areca palms shake convulsively in the sudden rain. Sunbathing gringos scatter like so many frightened piglets. One of the parrots spouts revolutionary poetry, surely trained by subversives at the hotel. Poetry by its very nature is subversive, Martín knows. It turns words inside out, confounds meaning, changes black-and-white to ambiguous shades of gray. *Never trust a poet.*

One of Martín's missions during the long civil war in his country was rooting out the intellectuals, the professors and university students, the decadent artists and actors and writers who made up a dangerous fringe of society. They identified with the plight of the peasants from their cozy armchairs, marched in a rally or two, spat at the police, then scuttled back to the safety of their hiding places. Martín took special satisfaction in flushing them out like vermin.

In detention, these so-called intellectuals exhibited no pride, no stamina like the campesinos they so staunchly defended. They responded to brute force best. In less than an hour, Martín would have them shitting their pants, betraying colleagues, turning in their *abuelitas* if they thought it would save their skins. They would sign false confessions, grovel like the cowering dogs they were. For all their fancy language and education, they were not real men. Real men had a tolerance for pain.

It's time for his squats, four sets of ten, two minutes rest in between. He's forty-three years old and in peak condition. He laughs to think of beating up a younger version of himself, at sixteen perhaps, when he joined the army at his father's behest. Severo Abel was the mayor of a village on the northern border, flexibly aligned with the powers that be. He'd tried to save Martín from forced conscription, a fate worse than the officer school where he ended up. As a new recruit, Martín was given a puppy to care for. He named his mutt Pipo and quickly grew to love him. After four months, he was ordered to kill the dog with his bare hands and eat its remains.

The colonel's stomach is unsettled, fermenting with the pork chops from lunch. God only knows what the kitchen workers did to his meat. *Carajo,* there isn't a soul in the world he can trust.

Even his wife betrayed him, took away his sons. Marisela lives in Connecticut now with her sister's family. His boys are becoming strangers to him, forgetting their Spanish, growing embarrassed about where they're from. Every day they're erasing him, their homeland, their own tongues. Antonio, the oldest, recently got his ear pierced and Calixto has taken up the flute. They'll turn into *maricones* if he doesn't save them soon.

Martín wishes his sons could grow up in the countryside, like he did. When the boys were small, they loved hearing stories about the ghost who haunted the river near his village. Everyone swore the ghost was the old butcher, Manny Panales, who liked to dress as a woman when he was alive. The villagers said Manny was thrown into the river by a passing soldier who mistook him for a hooker. When the soldier realized his mistake, he shot the butcher in the head.

After that, everyone learned to wade only knee-deep in the river to bathe, or wash clothes, or catch its tasty blue crabs. To venture any farther was to court misfortune. Martín nearly lost an eye once when a sliver of bone flew up from the river and tacked his left eyelid to his brow. (It sags a bit to this day.) Others disappeared and washed back to shore with holes in their skulls. Every New Year's Day, the villagers brought corn and trinkets and a clutch of festive feathers to the river to placate the butcher's spirit, but the vengeance didn't stop.

Martín's village had been rife with ugly rumors, including the one that he himself was a product of his mother's reputed affair with the deputy mayor, a skittish, close-shaven man with simian hands. Martín couldn't deny the fact that their noses—narrow at the base with delicate, flared nostrils—were both unusual and identical. But that singular detail didn't necessarily make them father and son. Another story had the village *bruja* telling his mother that she'd give birth to a girl who'd grow up to be a beauty queen. Martín was born instead.

From the corner of his good eye, the colonel spots the lady matador, cigar in hand, heading for the pool in a skimpy bikini. *¡Que cuerpo, por Dios!* She's more stunning than she looked in the elevator, dressed up in her suit of lights. Martín watches as she stubs out her cigar on the edge of the pool before executing a perfect dive. She stays underwater a full length, surfacing briefly before surging back toward the deep end. The woman is a nymph, a graceful extravagance. God put her on earth for no other purpose than to torment men. If she weren't a bullfighter, Martín thinks, she would make a perfect whore.

Martín sniffs his underarms. His hair and T-shirt are sweaty but he's otherwise presentable. If he takes the time to shower, he might miss her altogether. Martín pushes open the sliding glass doors of the gym and studies the lady matador's impeccable butterfly stroke. Perhaps she'll insist on a baroque dance of courtship, protocols of flower and song. No, she's a warrior like me, Martín decides, crouching by the pool. Before he can utter a word, the lady matador barks out like a seal. This surprises him, but the colonel is used to the unexpected in his line of work.

"So you've come to exhibit yourself here as well?" he teases her. She's doing the backstroke now, parting the water cleanly with her high-voltage spine. He can discern the weight of her nipples through her bikini top, hazelnuts almost too perfect to suck. He wants to jump in the pool and join her, see what happens next. Would the water electrocute them both?

The lady matador stands in the shallow end and faces the colonel. Her shoulders are square and strong. The air around them is agitated, a flock of furious birds.

"*Por favor, señorita.* Don't mistake me for one of your bulls." Martín stands and shields his heart in mock fear.

In response she holds up an imaginary cape, unsmiling. Martín is hypnotized by the sexy, twisted shell of her navel, and paws the ground with his bare feet. There is nothing but this, he thinks, this and only this.

The News

From Channel 9's *Top of the News*

Protesters in the highland village of Nojodes pelted the presidential forerunner, Senator Quiñonez, with garbage today when he interrupted their Sunday market. The peasants, who travel many miles on foot to sell their wares, complained that the senator's entourage had trampled their stalls without compensating them for damages. An angry goatherd set his flock loose on the surprised candidate. Let's turn now to the clip of the senator being chased down the mountainside . . .

From the Weather Channel

Tropical storm Odette crossed Trinidad and Tobago today, bringing torrential rains to the Caribbean islands and flooding villages along the Venezuelan coastline. Meteorologists predict the storm will gain force as it moves northward. Hurricane warnings are in effect in the Lesser Antilles and will likely spread to Puerto Rico, Cuba, and Central America. Stay tuned for more details . . .

From *La Boca Abierta,* a feminist radio program

Next Sunday, citizens will cast their votes for the presidency, the vice presidency, 159 members of Congress, twenty seats in the Central American parliament, and mayors for 331 municipalities. How many of these candidates are women? Exactly seven. How many have a serious chance of winning? Not one. We consider this a scandalous state of affairs.

At a recent forum of women congressional candidates sponsored by *La Boca Abierta,* the aspirants were asked what they would change about Congress. "Everything!" said Juanita Guerrero, who is campaigning for a seat in our easternmost district. If elected, she plans to implement a quota policy to ensure gender equity in Congress.

Reyna de León, a bakery owner in the capital, singled out corruption as the number one problem affecting parliamentary effectiveness. "We must put a stop to the cronyism and back-scratching that have paralyzed our country. Women must be the yeast for a change!"

Catarina Montejo, a law professor at San Francisco de Assisi University, emphasized that she would work to mainstream gender into public policies and push for stronger government response to issues of health, education, housing, and employment.

The ex-dictator's daughter, also a candidate for Congress, refused to participate in what she decried as a "sordid lesbian lovefest." Call her at home to express your displeasure at 232-4453 . . .

From *El Pajarito,* an astrology show

Ay, ay, ay, ay! My crystal ball is hazy today but I see clouds brewing on the horizon. Is it a hurricane, or the tempest of impending elections? A charismatic man with a beard is behind the dirty dealings. Whoever wears purple tomorrow will be protected from illness and the evil eye of jealous opponents. Do not wait another day to unburden yourself to the secret object of your affection. The clocks are chiming off-schedule so be sure you know the time . . .

From *La Estrella* magazine

In light of the upcoming presidential election, we posed this question to our country's most illustrious stars: Who do you most want to have dinner with at the National Palace?

Rigoberto Duarte, pop star: Oh dear, you know the last thing I am is a political animal! I guess I would sing for my supper if any of them asked me—nicely, of course. Do they know I'm pescatarian?

María Estefania Muñóz, soap opera star of *Forever Tomorrow:* The big question is not the presidents themselves but who their wives are—after all, they're the ones who'll make a dinner party a success.

Heberto Villanueva, game show host: Before anyone's elected or throwing state dinners, I think the presidential candidates should prove themselves as contestants on our human billiards show. Are you up for the challenge, gentlemen?

Lupe Galeano, talk show hostess: Well, I don't want to unduly affect the elections one way or another. But based on personal charm alone, I would have to choose that handsome devil from the Arriba Party. At the moment, though, I'm on a strict seven-hundred-calorie-a-day diet and not eating out whatsoever.

Alba "Frida" Montenegro, painter and performance artist: I've made my political views clear through my recent installation, *Puto Inválido*. Nothing could make me sit at the same table with that scum!

CHAPTER TWO

*An avalanche of press for the lady matador •
Orchids for the ex-guerrilla • The lawyer books a tour to Italy •
El coreano rejects a bolt of coarse cloth • The poet is robbed
at knifepoint • The news*

MONDAY

Life draws a tree
and death draws another one.

—Roberto Juarroz

The Ballroom

The lady matador is wearing yellow, the color of accidents and ill-omens, of bold overtures to gorings, and worse. She likes to tempt fate on the days she isn't fighting, bend superstition to her will. Wearing yellow will excite the journalists who are waiting for her in the rococo ballroom with their cameras and flashbulbs and rude, unyielding questions. Of course, they've heard of yellow's evil in the ring. It will announce to them: I dare to defy you, and you, and you.

Suki Palacios slips to the podium crowded with microphones. Her skintight *traje de luz* reflects the television lights. The crackle of high-wattage electricity at her lips pleases her. Silently, her *cuadrilla* forms a protective half ring behind her. These men, all Mexicans, have performed with her for over a year, enduring ridicule and insults for backing a woman in the ring. Suki waits, savoring the frantic scene before her, imagining that the ballroom is underwater and the journalists skittish fish she could dispatch in an instant.

She selects a bespectacled man in the back for her first question.

"Why do you do it, Suki? Why do you fight the bulls?"

"Because they are there," she answers, paraphrasing Mallory's remark about wanting to climb Mount Everest. Suki twists the turquoise ring on her middle finger, the one she's convinced stopped a charging bull in Monterrey.

"Do you consider yourself a feminist?" asks a TV reporter.

"If that means I get to choose, then yes, I'm a feminist."

"Choose what?" several journalists shout out.

"Choose what I do with my life." Suki wants to add: and which bulls I kill, and which men I fuck, and how I die. She thinks of reporters as a necessary evil, bottom-feeders, rotten to the core. If she were forced into cannibalism, she'd eat their flesh last.

"Why are you wearing yellow?" someone barks. "Aren't you superstitious?"

"I like to tempt fate." Suki strikes a photo-worthy pose, hands on hips, as if inviting challengers. The harsh TV lights make her long for the old-fashioned river lanterns in Japan. Suki was four years old when her mother first took her to visit her grandmother in Yokohama. A festival was under way and the river near her *oma*'s house softly glowed with lit boats all night long. The memory tempers the lady matador's mood.

"Tell us about yesterday's fight," asks a man in a Panama hat.

"What's there to tell?" She shrugs. "The bull was small, too meek. I hope you can come up with better *toros* than that."

"Aren't you afraid of death?" The question comes from a beefy woman wearing overlapping headsets.

"Tell me how you die and I'll tell you how you've lived." Suki heard a renowned poet say this once. She liked how it sounded but she didn't really believe it. Her mother's life couldn't have pointed to her sad collapse. The year before Mamá died, she shrank thirteen inches, her joints turned to dust in their sockets—and she was petite to begin with. No, Suki thinks, death couldn't begin to define her.

"What are your weaknesses?" asks a bald man loaded down with recording equipment.

"Hairless men," she retorts, straight-faced, and the audience howls.

"Look at me!" the reporter next to him jokes, ripping open his shirt to reveal a smooth chest.

"Do your fans ever give you trouble?" an über-coiffed anchorwoman asks.

"Sometimes they lunge at me worse than the bulls," Suki deadpans to more laughter.

"As a *matadora,* you are both beloved and despised. How do you account for this disparity?" This question seems to come out of nowhere but Suki knows it's a crucial one to address.

"We fear what we love most," she says. The room grows quiet

as Suki lets this sink in. Then she smoothes her hair and grins. "And we *especially* love what we fear."

The journalists roar their approval.

"Will you go back to your studies?" someone else shouts.

"Perhaps when I'm through in the ring." Suki dropped out of medical school in Los Angeles to prepare for her debut in Tijuana. She still carries around her first-year anatomy book with its garish pink organs and plastic page dividers.

"They say you have no manager. Are you looking for one?"

"Since my father retired, I've decided to manage myself. There's already too much testosterone in my life as it is."

Suki turns and blows a kiss to the five men in her *cuadrilla,* handsome in their bullfighting finery. Her father's family in Veracruz called in old favors to assemble them. In fact, it was Tía Chofi, youngest sister of Abuelo Ramón, who arranged Suki's training with the top toreadors in Puebla and Guadalajara. In the extant world of bullfighting, Tía Chofi ensures that the Palacios name remains golden. Never mind that El Azteca was dead a good ten years before Suki was born.

"People say you're violent. Is that true?" The lights blind her and she can't tell who asked the question.

"Only when necessary." Suki checks her watch. In her experience, too much time with reporters is worse than too little.

"Are you looking forward to battling your nemesis?"

"Paloma Gómez is a fine competitor."

The last time she crossed paths with La Paloma, the latter called Suki a mongrel and spat at her feet. Suki's response: *¡Pues, que viva el mongrel!* Paloma and five other *matadoras* will converge on the tropical capital to compete for the first women's bullfighting title in Latin America: Lety Betancourt from Venezuela,

Hortensia Pacheco from Bolivia, the Colombian twins Laura and Trinidad de Morales, Jesusa Fernández from Peru.

"What will you do with the prize money if you win?"

"*When* I win, I plan to donate half the proceeds to medical research." Not that Suki needs the winnings. An inheritance from her Japanese grandmother left her financially comfortable for at least a decade. She wonders what her mother and *oma* would think of her fighting the bulls.

"I'll take two more questions." Suki glances around for a man who might meet her requirements for the day. "Yes, over there, with the green turtleneck."

The journalist identifies himself as Abelardo Valenzuela, the editor of a local literary magazine. "If you could be any smell in the world, what would it be?"

The hot stink of a charging bull is what first comes to mind but the lady matador pauses before answering. Her nostrils distend with the memory of cherished scents. The cyclamen in her mother's garden. Her *oma's* rice-dust face powder. The *tostones* her father fried up for her in Veracruz after a grueling afternoon in the ring. And, of course, the drugstore perfumes worn by the gang girls in East L.A. When Suki was little, she wanted to grow up and become a Chicana. Those women took no shit from anyone.

"Burning sugarcane," she retorts, inciting a chorus of wolf whistles.

Suki calls on her last questioner, a spindly man in a suit and tie who waves his arm like a censer.

"Do you have a personal motto?" he asks.

"*Sí.*" Suki cocks her thumb and forefinger at him. "If I aim, move." She poses for photographs with her *cuadrilla,* signs autographs, waves away further questions. Then with a bow to the white-hot lights, she disappears.

Suki huddles with her men, thanking them for their patience. They aren't the standard coterie of fighters, but what they lack in virtuosity they make up in loyalty. She loves them like brothers. Three of the five, in fact, are related to her: Manolo and Paco Iturralde, her trusted *banderilleros,* are second cousins, as is Octavio, who doubles as her sword boy. And her picadors, Luís Granados and Melvyn Sánchez, come from bullfighting families of picadors in Veracruz. The five of them have vowed to stay together, for better or worse, until Suki quits the ring.

The lady matador opens the minibar in her hotel room and pours herself a double vodka, no ice. Then she orders a rare steak from room service. The vodka burns her throat cleanly, drifts down between her legs. Suki considers the colonel from yesterday, inflated with muscles, stomping the ground like a novice bull. He seemed to expect her to fuck him right there in the pool. In the year and a half since she's been fighting professionally, Suki knows what works best for her: a simple man, not too intelligent, grateful and discreet.

She ignores the lavish bouquet of Amazon lilies delivered to her room. Perhaps one of the journalists sent them, though they're usually too cheap for this degree of splurge. It's better that she doesn't know the sender. This way she'll treat him no better or worse than anyone else. Nothing drives a man crazier, faster, than a lack of acknowledgment. Rejected suitors have accused Suki of sadism, and worse. The fact is, she prefers to do the pursuing herself.

The doorbell rings and Suki lets in the waiter—skinny, clean-shaven, a bit pale for her taste. He's wearing a waistcoat and pants too short by an inch. She watches him set down her order on the ostentatious desk.

"Take off your shoes," she demands.

"I beg your pardon?"

"Your socks, too. Do it now."

The young man flushes but complies.

Suki signs the check, tipping him no more generously than usual, and points to her sword. "If you breathe a word of this to anyone, I'll skewer you."

Then smiling, she pulls him to her bed.

"My name's M—"

"I don't need to know your name, *querido*." Suki loosens her bathrobe and permits the waiter a glimpse of her breasts. He looks stricken, frozen to the spot. She takes his wrist and guides his hand past the terry-cloth lapel.

"May I lay my head there?" His voice quavers like a boy's.

Nobody has ever asked her this before. The lady matador slips off her robe and displays herself for the young waiter. He removes a tiny gold cross on a chain from around his neck and tucks it into a back pocket. Then carefully, as if he were nestling against porcelain, he rests his cheek on her breast, giving off a faint pot roast scent. He remains there, breathing so steadily that Suki fears he's fallen asleep.

When he licks her throat without warning, Suki is surprised at his feral strength. Then he reaches down and caresses her ribs, her belly, the curve of her hip. His hands are large and calloused and they scrape her upper thighs. He inserts a finger deep inside her, and Suki moans. She feels his hardness against her waist and reaches down to release him. Before she can take him into her mouth, he lifts her and positions her on his face.

"Pull back your lips," he whispers.

With both hands, Suki pushes back her moist tangle of hair and spreads the folds—gleaming, pink, slick. The waiter drags his tongue across her wilderness. She watches. She's never thought of the tongue as a gorgeous muscle before. The shuddering begins in the tip of the waiter's tongue and flashes through Suki, branched lightning illuminating her body. *Ay, sí.* She could light up the night sky with her pleasure.

When Suki turns to her lover again, he's already straightening his jacket and zipping his pants, fastening the gold chain with the tiny cross back around his neck. He dabs at his mouth with a freshly pressed handkerchief, extracted from the same pocket. Suki notices a scar beneath his left earlobe, raised and notched as a caterpillar. She lowers her gaze and gets a long, last look at his splendid feet before he puts on his socks and slightly battered black shoes.

When the young man is ready to leave, he bows deeply, a concert bow. The peacocks screech in the gardens below. "It has been my honor to serve you, señorita."

Roof

It's been nearly a year since the ex-guerrilla received flowers from her dead brother. Today's orchid is five-petaled, like an outstretched hand, neon yellow with rust-colored spots. Two more blossoms—one pink, one red—are stacked at its center, just above the stem. Aura Estrada no longer questions how Julio manages to get the orchids to her at the hotel. The accompanying note instructs her to meet him on the roof at noon. Julio claims that Aura's longing conjures him from infinity. But she's been trying to reach him these last few months without success. Then out of the blue, Julio chooses the busiest time of day for them to meet. Most likely, he's trying to get her fired. He never did want her working at the hotel.

Aura takes the elevator to the top floor then. Her pink-and-white uniform provides the necessary camouflage. No one will question her carrying this tray of sugar buns and tea. She passes the octogenarian actress who lives in the west penthouse suite and orders ice with grenadine syrup for breakfast. The actress, quite emaciated, is wearing cream silk pajamas and her customary ostrich boa, and has her triplet Chihuahuas in tow. Aura greets the woman but she's drifting in a world of her own. Aura climbs the last flight of stairs and shoulders open the roof's emergency door. The alarm doesn't sound. Her brother probably arranged this, too.

It takes a moment for her eyes to adjust to the noon light. The city looks different from the rooftop, as if the buildings and trees, even the cathedral itself, were suspended by a menacing grid of wires. From here she can see the colorful tents of the marketplace, the shoeshine boys with their polishes and brushes. If everything were turned upside down, would the people on the bottom end up on top? Not a chance, Aura thinks. The rich would still find a way to reign.

The air is acrid, hemmed in by the surrounding mountains. Smoke rises from the city dump. A thunderstorm builds in the distance. Aura worries that the tar on the roof will stain her white, crepe-soled shoes. She sets down her tray, emptying her mind, and waits. Julio arrives differently each time—on a gust of wind, in the plaintive call of a mourning dove, with the shifting, whispering leaves. Once he was a ring of blue encircling a disembodied voice; another time, the ache between her shoulder blades. Sometimes she forgets what he looked like alive.

Reliving Julio's last moments often coaxes him to return. The images are there behind Aura's eyelids, waiting to be replayed. The soldiers with their torches. The captain, indicating with a jut of his chin that their cornfield be burned. Their family's plot was modest, barely enough to feed them all—Mamá, Cristina and Telma, Julio, and her. The day the soldiers came, it hadn't rained in a month. The corn took to the fire eagerly, crackling and popping, offering itself to heaven. Julio stood watching their field burn to the ground until he could bear it no longer.

Before anyone could stop him, he rushed into the field and tried to put out the flames with a blanket. The soldiers pointed at him and laughed. Only the captain wasn't amused. He ordered his men to surround the plot. How her brother danced, trying to outrun the fire! But the soldiers refused to let him escape. Julio leaped into the air like he was taking wing—his ribs etched in flames, his arms straining heavenward, his neck extended like a hissing goose. Aura prayed that he would fly, join the black-throated jay in the ceiba tree. Instead he fell to the ground, his skin charred and smoking, dying miserably in what was left of their corn.

In the years following his death, Aura worshipped her brother like a saint. Everything she did was refracted through that wall of flames. Every sacrifice she made, she offered up to him.

A sudden rustling catches her attention. It's Julio, his scrawny flanks scattering leaves.

"There you are," she whispers, afraid that listening to her brother will erase everything that isn't him.

"Perdóname," he says, flicking off leaves. "I've been busy."

"So even the dead are busy these days." Aura grins. "I've brought you sugar buns and tea. Drink. It will give you strength."

"Thank you."

Aura bites into a bun, licking the sugar from her lips. A few errant raindrops prick her forehead. "Are you still fourteen, Julio? Or have you gotten old like me?" she asks playfully. "Tell me, are angels ageless?"

"Shhhhh, *hermana.* I haven't come for games."

"What is it then?"

"He's among us."

"Who?" Aura tries the tea, wishing she'd brewed the cinnamon kind instead.

"El asesino."

"There are so many here, Julio. The hotel is full of them."

"The one who killed me, who burned our field."

"The captain?"

"Yes, except he's a colonel now. You served him pork chops yesterday."

Aura tries to pinpoint his face. Then she sees him: yes, the one with the cartoon muscles and sunglasses sitting with the Americans. Her throat tightens.

"Do you remember him now?" Julio asks.

She recalls the other villagers killed by the captain's soldiers that day. The thief's head bashed in with the butt of a rifle. The Gutierrez brothers shot at point-blank range. The baby girl kicked around like a soccer ball in her christening gown. For good measure, they slaughtered the mayor's horse and left it to rot in the sun. That day, Aura went from being fatherless to being brotherless and, the following winter, to being motherless after Mamá died from grief.

Aura had been her mother's last miracle, born after four miscarriages in as many years. The curandera from across the river had advised Mamá to wear a white loincloth—*like the one Jesus Christ Himself wore on the cross*—under her skirts to catch her next child. The following spring, Mamá "caught" her in a field of green, grass-scented corn. After her mother died, Aura and her older sisters were left to fight the mongrels for scraps. Eventually, Cristina and Telma pledged themselves to the church but Aura refused. Instead she joined the guerrillas.

During the long civil war, Aura lost her lover, Juan Carlos, to the same enemy. How she missed the woolly smell of his wet fatigues in the jungle. The pride he took in his foul iguana stew. The way he held himself back until she took her pleasure, then sang her to sleep with nonsense lullabies. The curve of his arms, his chin, his cock.

"There's a place in the universe where memories are written down, where nothing is forgotten." Her brother's voice sounds dust-dry. "Send him to me, *hermana*."

"Me? How?"

"Tú sabes cómo."

Aura knocks over her tea. "I don't do that anymore."

After she left the jungle, her sisters tried to cure her of rage. With permission from their superiors, Cristina and Telma took her into their cool, stone convent for ten months. They locked up Aura's pistol, forced her to sleep in a feathered bed, polished the chapel's floor with their entreaties. Aura memorized the morning liturgy but refused confession altogether. Her nightmares persisted. She flinched with the memories of mines and artillery fire, nursed her thirst for revenge. The rage returns when she least expects it, disrupting the labored years of forgetting.

The first time Aura killed a man, it was easier than she thought. She surprised the soldier from behind and, incredibly, he didn't resist. His blood didn't seem real to her, nor did the look of disbelief on his face. Only his lips, ill defined as ground meat, reminded her of why she'd come. He'd raped eleven girls in as many days. That was all she knew. No, that soldier wasn't difficult to kill. Yet with each succeeding one, it got harder.

Now it's Julio who wants revenge. His killer is at the hotel, eating pork chops prepared in her kitchen. Isn't that why she'd joined the guerrillas in the first place? To hunt that bastard down? *Use any means at your disposal.* That's what the revolutionary Cuban pamphlets taught her. There were rules for every form of resistance and subterfuge. *Fight violence with violence; fear with more fear.* Pages of rationalizations marching as inspiration. *A righteous end justifies the means.*

"Thanks for the tea." Julio's voice is weakening, overtaken by the wild parakeets in the ficus tree. "Next time bring me hot chocolate, okay?"

Aura feels depleted, as if she's lost an entire night's sleep. With each visit, her brother siphons off another measure of her strength. More Cuban rules swim in her head. She'd banish them from her head altogether if Juan Carlos hadn't uttered them like prayers.

It's five minutes to noon. Aura is no longer surprised at Julio's tricks of time. At least nobody will have missed her in the kitchen. She considers her brother's intent. Whatever she does, she loses. And she's sick and tired of losing. Aura rushes across the roof and through the emergency door, trying to shake off the stupor engulfing her, taking the stairs two at a time down the sixteen stories to the ground floor, committing the day's specials to memory.

Appetizers: tortilla soup, ceviche
Main courses: fried steak smothered in onions; tilapia with rice and *maduros*
Dessert: coconut flan, chocolate fudge cake, apple pie

The Atrium

The shopping atrium is teeming with the frivolous matrons the lawyer detests. Gertrudis Stüber looks them over with a disapproving eye. Two of them, ridiculously, are wearing imported fox fur stoles. When the new shipment of clothing arrives from Miami every Monday, the women viciously battle each other over the finery. The hotel shop owners know better than to order more than one of anything. Gertrudis avoids the melee by shopping in Italy. Last spring she returned with red lizard boots, sweaters soft as moths, envy-inspiring cashmere suits.

The lawyer doesn't feel her usual sense of triumph after a morning's testimony before Congress. Los Mohosos—the moldy ones, her catchall name for her political adversaries—are lobbying to abolish private adoptions and put the government in charge. A politician on Gertrudis's payroll had the audacity to condemn foreign adoptions, citing that Korea had stopped exporting its babies. "It's imperative that we follow suit," Senator Silvestre Jiménez demanded. "Are we any less of a culture?"

His tirade wasn't about saving children but about making money—and boosting his sagging popularity with a distracting new cause. He and the other politicians want a bigger cut of the lucrative adoption business under the guise of more regulation. They couldn't be more transparent. The lawyers, equally transparent and led by Gertrudis, are fighting to preserve their profits. As far as she's concerned, there's no downside to sending a fraction of the country's underprivileged children overseas. Nothing awaits them here but misery.

After her testimony, lobbyists of every persuasion surrounded Gertrudis, vying for her attention in competing clouds of brilliantine. She estimates that her payroll will swell considerably by week's end. There is nothing real about realpolitik here. Everything masquerades as something else.

At the hotel travel agency, Fabio Morabito—flamboyantly dressed in purple—races to greet her. Fabio plans every detail of Gertrudis's annual trips to Florence, down to her appointments at the exclusive shops near the Ponte Vecchio. The travel agent is also charged with procuring escorts for *la abogada*. In nine years of following his recommendations, she's never been disappointed. A photograph of Michelangelo's *David* hangs in the agency. He's the model from which Fabio works to find her companions.

"I have everything for you right here," Fabio purrs, patting a leather portfolio. His stereo oozes Rigoberto Duarte's latest hit, "Give Me Back My Heart."

"Please keep this on my same account."

"A sus órdenes, Doctora."

"What's the news today?" Nobody knows more about the goings-on at the hotel than this little travel agent. Information peels off him like an orange rind.

"The lady matador had a press conference and all hell broke loose!"

"Oh?"

"Have you seen her? She's very, very beautiful. The reporters are making fools of themselves."

"And the military conference?" The lawyer pays no mind to younger women unless they work for her.

Fabio leans in conspiratorially, adjusting his silk foulard. "There were two bomb scares this morning."

"Security is tight?"

"Any tighter and they couldn't walk!" He laughs shrilly but stops when the lawyer doesn't share his mirth. "You have just the one baby here right now?"

"Yes, but I'm expecting another soon." Gertrudis is concerned. Her best breeder mother is overdue by three weeks and insists she wants to keep the child already promised to a couple from Tennessee. "You'll stay informed?"

"Count on me." Fabio raises his eyebrows until they practically merge with his hairline. "Did you hear that *el pajarito* predicted a hurricane?"

"You don't believe that clown, do you?" Gertrudis inspects her manicure.

"I've been keeping track of his predictions, and fifty percent of them come true."

"Those aren't exceptional odds, Fabio."

"Yes, but to live your life even half right seems extraordinary to me!"

"My trip to Florence will be a hundred percent right, no?" Gertrudis glances again at the photograph of the *David*.

"Absolutely, Doctora." And with a bow, Fabio walks her to the door.

The lawyer sits in the garden restaurant and consults her leather date book. She has back-to-back appointments with legislators, a speech at the civil lawyers union, and a hairdresser's appointment at five. Gertrudis checks her watch, exasperated. Her husband is already twenty-seven minutes late. It's unreasonable for him to insist on meeting her here in the middle of the day.

Hans finally shows up at 12:49. He's a giant, taller than her by six inches. Gertrudis is struck, as she often is, by his easy grace. It's impressive how someone so big pulls off such delicate gestures. She's been married to him for seventeen years, twelve of them celibate. Divorce is out of the question. At her age it would appear ridiculous, a sign of instability.

"I don't have much time." The lawyer finishes her coffee and signals the waitress for a refill. In the garden, flycatchers flit among the bamboo.

"A cheese-and-salsa omelet and a double side of bacon," Hans orders in his high-pitched voice.

The ensuing silence, minutes long, forces Gertrudis to study her husband's face. He's aging well—better than she is, if truth be told, and he's five years older. It's been decades since anybody called her beautiful but she was striking in her youth, and a few daring men were drawn to her, including the brilliant revolutionary who left her for the French ambassador's wife. The lawyer doesn't delude herself. She knows there's a vanishing point for everything: beauty, sympathy, even love.

Hans looks ill at ease. The last thing she wants is another one of his soul-searching confessions. Certainly, her husband doesn't need any tired justifications for his actions. They have an arrangement, a good one, and Gertrudis has been exceedingly generous about his failings. She even ignored his very public fling last year with that two-bit soap opera star from *Forever Tomorrow*. It dominated the gossip pages for months, resuscitating María what's-her-name's career. Gertrudis is bored by Hans dragging her through his affairs. She wouldn't dream of burdening him with the details of her own indiscretions.

"It's different this time," he begins.

"I don't want to hear about it."

"It concerns you."

"Not if I don't care."

"I'm in love—"

"I said I don't care."

"—with one of the mothers," Hans says flatly, shrugging his massive shoulders.

Gertrudis sets down her cup and wills herself to breathe normally. She goes through her inventory of breeder mothers, stopping short at Danila. Why didn't she see this coming?

"It's your baby then?" Her mouth tightens around the words.

"It's—"

"I know who it is."

Hans picks up his fork. With the dainty movement of a tea party matron, he takes a bite of his omelet. The pale hairs on his knuckles gleam. His Adam's apple bobs in his disturbingly smooth throat. What would it take to rip it out?

"I can't afford a scandal," Gertrudis says evenly. Separate lives, yes. Separate sex, yes. Falling in love, no. Jeopardizing her business interests, definitely not. She won't abide such disorder.

Her husband's face reddens. "Love doesn't have—"

"You will not shame me in public," Gertrudis cuts him off. "You will not undermine my business in any way." The cold mechanics of his betrayal heighten her lucidity. "This is between me and you. That breeder means nothing." She'll bury the two of them alive if she has to, shovel the dirt herself. I am master here, she thinks.

Hans devours eight strips of bacon, buttered toast, the remains of his omelet, and a large pineapple juice. Then he scrapes, almost tenderly, a bit of onion off his plate. He drinks three cups of coffee with sugar and extra cream.

A month ago they got into a ridiculous argument over their childhoods, of all things, which they'd largely spent together. Hans accused Gertrudis of being cold, of not crying when her mother was bucked off a horse and killed. But that wasn't true. After the funeral, Gertrudis buried herself in her mother's lustrous riding clothes, inhaling the lingering scents for days. This was how she'd grieved—utterly alone.

Hans folds his napkin and places it beside his plate. His blond hair, Gertrudis notices, is more streaked with gray than she remembers. Arguments tumble through her brain: if, then, if, then, if. Bottom line: How much will it take to pay him off?

"That child is spoken for. I have a deposit already," she starts again.

"I'll ruin you." Her husband flattens his hands against the table.

"Damn it, Hans, I help those children. God is—"

"God is drunk and in the forest breaking all the rules."

"Hans, please."

"Let's not aggrandize ourselves, Gertrudis." Her husband stands up. His enormous hands hang loosely at his side. There's an expression on his face she hasn't seen before. Could he really be in love?

A part of her wants to sell off every gestating baby in her inventory and move to Florence, spend her days gazing at the

David. What does she care if her husband goes off with some peasant? She'll leave them both destitute in the end. But the rest of her wants revenge.

Elevator

Killing himself is not the first thing on Won Kim's mind when he wakes up but it soon becomes the day's imperative. By the time he arrives at the Glorious Textiles factory, his workers are loudly arguing. They disagree about many things, mostly over who will be saved—half of his employees are Catholic; the other half vehemently evangelical. Heaven is a long way off, Won Kim wants to tell them. Normally he circumvents their ecclesiastical disputes with competitions that increase productivity. Nine times out of ten, the evangelicals win.

Today his workers are fighting over something else entirely: an article in *El Nuevo Tiempo*. Won Kim does not read the newspapers nor watch much television. During his rare free time he still enjoys collecting butterflies. The grainy, front-page photograph of himself catches Won Kim off guard. The allegations are multitudinous: that he pays his workers next to nothing; that he permits no breaks in a ten-hour workday; that he interrogates employees about their reproductive plans and fires mothers-to-be.

Like complaints from a crazy old uncle, there is a grain of truth to each claim. But the charges are grossly disproportionate to his crimes. His father, who was guilty of infinitely more egregious offenses, never had his integrity questioned. (It was rumored that he had drunkenly sired children from here to Argentina.) Won Kim sighs. He feels unspeakably fatigued.

"Whatever happened to Filomena?" the Catholic ringleader demands.

"And the other girls who were fired?" the evangelicals chime in. For once these bitter rivals are in accord, united against him.

"I can assure you, ladies, these accusations are baseless," Won Kim insists, but a slight waver in his voice emboldens them.

"Why don't we hear from anyone after they leave?" asks Mireya Hernández, who has been trying to unionize the workers since spring.

"I cannot account for the social inclinations of my former employees," Won Kim snaps. "Now everyone get back to work, or I will instate these false claims as the factory's new rules."

The women shuffle back to their places, grumbling. They know his factory is the best maquiladora on the strip. Won Kim guesses that the newspaper rounded up the worst hearsay from all the factories and applied them, most dramatically, to his. Yes, he pays his workers less than minimum wage (one-third less, as a matter of fact) and their breaks are not long (only fifteen minutes twice a day). But it is still better than working in the coffee fields or picking corn.

Generally, Won Kim ignores what his fellow countrymen are doing. He interacts with them at the monthly meeting of the Korean Manufacturers' Association, no more. Brutish and money-grubbing to the last, punctuating their sentences with expectorant, they are repugnant to Won Kim. They are the sort of men, he supposes, his father would have championed as models of masculinity.

All his life, Won Kim endured his father's litany of charges against him. That he was too delicate for a boy, prone to girlish tears. That he dabbled in unacceptable pursuits—butterflies, and daydreaming, and solitude. Even unconsciousness was no refuge from the rebukes. Once, his father accused him of dreaming so hard that his whole body shook. What sort of real boy did that?

Won Kim retreats to his office, separated from the factory floor by a thick pane of glass. It is not easy pretending to work in this aquarium, soundlessly magnified and on display. An hour lasts a century and still he cannot concentrate. His father's portrait hangs opposite his desk, scowling at him, exhorting him to action. He dismisses the option of getting rid of the painting. It does not matter that his father is four years dead. His admonishments persist even from the grave. Won Kim's shame sours and twists inside him. He leaves the Catholic ringleader in charge and gets in his car, heading toward the capital.

Perhaps his mistress told someone of her predicament. It is tempting to blame Berta for everything: his misery, his self-absorption, his regrets for things undone. But she is a mere girl. Her oddities and skittishness have bloomed in seclusion, and he alone is responsible. Won Kim envies the courage of those who live according to their own dictates, or choose to abandon life in a blaze of glory. His father had done this.

As Won Kim makes his way downtown, the sounds of the city seem far off to him. He grows dismayed by the plethora of election posters. One candidate is worse than the next, beginning and ending with that ex-dictator. The vulgarity everywhere oppresses him. If he's lucky, he'll swerve into a ditch.

A sudden downpour drenches the city. Near La Plazuela España, a beggar family hunches in a doorway, a filthy infant in its mother's arms. Vendors of every stripe are fighting to stay alive. One of them, a bowlegged *indígeno,* thrusts a bolt of coarse cloth through Won Kim's open window. Won Kim crashes his car onto the sidewalk, provoking a flood of curses from passersby.

"No! I told you no!" he screams at the vendor, who is only encouraged by the exchange. Exasperated, Won Kim reaches into his pocket and thrusts a bill into the man's hand. "Just go away. Keep your damn cloth."

Won Kim's plan crystallizes as he approaches the hotel. He will tell his mistress that he is taking the day off to drive her to the beach, the one where they saw the baby turtles hatch last spring. When they reach the ocean, he will suggest driving farther, to Puerto Verde, where the deep-sea fishing boats are docked. The fish are large and plentiful off the coast, Won Kim will say, and many records have been set in its waters.

Berta will not want to go. She will complain about seasickness, her inability to swim, how the ocean frightens her. Won Kim is determined to prevail. He must. He will select the finest boat in the fleet, one festooned with international flags. Once aboard, he will offer the captain a bottle of scotch, feign interest in the fishing equipment, help his mistress bait her line. When they are far out to sea and the captain is safely drunk, Won Kim will push Berta overboard. Then he will follow her.

Won Kim puts on his sunglasses as he enters the hotel lobby. Fake Greek statuary bookend the brass reception desk. He considers ordering a meal in the garden restaurant. That pretty waitress is on shift today, the one with the graceful hips who cheerfully refills his tea. A man planning suicide should not be thinking of his stomach, he scolds himself, but he cannot help it. He wishes his mother could prepare his favorite dish for him one last time:

ground pork with sesame oil and chili peppers, hotbed chives fried up with dried clams, crisp and tasty, over a mound of sticky rice.

How sick he is of tortillas!

The elevators are slow in coming, ticking erratically like broken metronomes. The doors of one finally open and the lady matador emerges smoking a cigar, magnificently, against hotel rules. What would a woman like that cost to bed, Won Kim wonders— that is, *if* she had a price? In his twelve years in the capital, he has never gone to a bullfight, much less to one featuring a woman. He does not doubt the lady matador's skills, or any woman's for that matter. Why, he would place odds on his own mother triumphing in the ring.

A second elevator opens, disgorging the tall man who greeted him yesterday. *"Buenas tardes,"* he says. "How's your wife?"

"Bien, bien. Gracias." Won Kim does not want to engage this man, or anyone for that matter.

"Coño, I forgot something." The tall man rushes back to the elevator and slips in.

They glide upward at what seems, to Won Kim, a glacial pace. He pretends to study the fabric between the elevator's wood paneling—a cheap polyester blend patterned with royal palms. Then he looks up at the partially mirrored ceiling, hoping to avoid a conversation. The fluorescent lights are decidedly unflattering. He looks colorless, lifeless, already dead.

"I'm Ricardo Morán, poet at large, exile from Cuba, anti-Communist, former political prisoner. And, if I do say so myself, a fine bolero dancer." He holds out his hand. "And you are?"

Won Kim shakes his hand limply but says nothing.

"Ah, you must be Korean. A businessman, I presume? You

know, our two countries have much in common. Bitterly divided by politics. Pawns of the United States. I've always thought of Koreans as the Cubans of Asia."

"Is that so?" Won Kim bristles. "And I've always thought of Cubans as the Koreans of the Caribbean."

The elevator stops almost imperceptibly between the seventh and eighth floors. There is no dramatic lurching or screeching of metal. In the vast wheel of fate, Won Kim laments, why is it his lot to be trapped in an elevator with this buffoon?

"You have the perspicacity of a scientist, I can see that," the Cuban persists.

Won Kim is annoyed for being pleased. He reminds himself that he is under no compulsion to speak to this man.

"Whom do you read for pleasure?" the poet asks, ignoring Won Kim's indifference. "Are you familiar with the works of Charles Darwin?"

"Yes, I am." In fact, Won Kim translated *On the Origin of Species* into Korean during the miserable year he spent at business school. It helped keep him sane. But if he were really sane, he would not have ended up in these hellish tropics planning to drown himself and his mistress. The curtain rose on his life long ago, he thinks, and what did he do? Scurry offstage to hide in the wings.

"Reading is the most effective barricade against hopelessness, don't you agree?" Ricardo asks, perspiration dampening his temples.

A butterfly, Won Kim wants to retort, *is the only reliable song against sorrow.* But he says nothing. As if on cue, the elevator light goes off. A disconcerting buzz envelops them.

"Damn it to hell," Won Kim mutters.

"Interrupted plans?" The poet's voice bounces off the elevator walls, reverberating everywhere at once. His breathing sounds forced, louder than it should.

"As a matter of fact," Won Kim says, "I was planning to kill myself."

Back Alley

The poet decides to take the stairs after the debacle of the broken elevator. Fifty-six minutes he waited for the repairmen to come and set him free. Fifty-six minutes of heat and stress and airlessness. Fifty-six minutes in the company of that morbid Korean businessman who refused to look at him or to say another word after his desperate pronouncement. Ricardo tried everything to draw him out, if only to calm his own nerves, but making conversation with a head of cabbage would've been easier.

He wonders whether *el coreano* really intended to kill himself, or only said it for dramatic effect. In his darkest days, imprisoned on the Isle of Pines and up to his neck in degenerates, suicide didn't occur to him. He was spellbound even by that misshapen world.

Ricardo stops at the garden restaurant and orders a lemonade to go. The same waitress who took care of him Sunday procures his drink. Her name tag reads AURA. Ricardo likes the way the waitress moves, so femininely anchored in her hips, and he finds her hairnet sexy, an intriguing little web.

"*Gracias, Señor Morán.*"

"*A usted, señorita.*" Ricardo is no longer surprised that everyone in the hotel knows his name. Perhaps job applicants are rigorously tested for memory as part of the hiring process. He imagines prospective waiters, housekeepers, and doormen being shown a hundred faces and names in quick succession. Any applicant with an instant recall of 95 percent or better gets the job.

The smell of a cigar, a good Cuban one, wafts toward Ricardo. A ribbon of smoke rises from the jungle orchids in the garden. It's the lady matador. Ricardo wants to speak to her but doesn't want to appear ill-mannered. He elbows his way past a cluster of amaryllis. The lady matador's back is turned to him. She's wearing a stretchy unitard with provocative leopard spots.

"Do I smell a Cohiba?" Ricardo ventures amiably. It's El Comandante's preferred cigar, though he purportedly gave them up years ago.

The bullfighter doesn't answer him, only blows more smoke in the air with a sultry tilt of her head. He wants to ask her if she's ever considered suicide, to tell her about the businessman in the elevator. Or maybe invite her to dance to the piped-in bolero (decidedly second-rate) and watch her hips shift to the rhythm. Ricardo remembers that the lady matador is part Japanese and so he scours his memory for a snatch of pertinent poetry.

"Sadness / A half-peeled apple / not a metaphor / Not a poem / Merely there," he recites.

This gets her attention and she turns around, a hand on her slender waist. "What do you know about it?"

"I know too well its melancholy gaze." He notices her fingernails, the cuticles chewed and bleeding.

The lady matador looks him over, lingering, it seems to Ricardo, on his oversized feet. A blowtorch couldn't have singed him more.

"Are you married?"

The question catches him by surprise. Why would a woman like her, a slayer of bulls, a wearer of leopard spots, give a damn about convention?

"It's complicated," he mutters. Ricardo wants to complain about his wife but can't pinpoint anything blatant enough. Since he's been married, he's had two short-lived affairs—a paltry record by Cuban standards.

"Answer me."

"Yes, I am."

She smiles with perfect, carnivorous teeth. Perhaps he should offer up his hand for her to chew.

"Get lost." Her voice is pleasant. The ash on her cigar drifts to the ground, a tiny swoon of gray.

"I beg your pardon?"

"I said get lost," she repeats without a hint of aggression.

This disarms him so completely that he bows and backs away. This must be how she dispatches her bulls. No wonder the woman is notorious in the ring. Most likely, the lady matador hates men. This is why she's so intent on slaying the ultimate symbol of virility. Ricardo wonders if he's irreversibly drawn to emasculating women. Most likely his affliction began with his mother, who accused him of sucking her breasts dry until he was three. To wean him, she'd had to coat her nipples with chili powder and smack him repeatedly on the head. To her dying day, Mami blamed him for her collapsed tits.

The poet is in no mood for the liveried lackeys in the lobby, especially that unctuous concierge with the engraved name tag. Right now, Ricardo longs to be anonymous. He takes what he thinks is a side door to the street into the steamy laundry room, bustling with uniformed workers washing, ironing, and folding mountains of clothes. The place is cavernous, windowless, like a factory from the Industrial Age. Ricardo spots a seamstress with tomato red pincushions and a rainbow's worth of spooled thread who reminds him of his ex-wife. The bulky overseer, sweating under his white bandanna, finally points Ricardo toward the back door.

In the fetid alley behind the hotel, a young tough brushes past the poet, then pushes him against a brick wall. He makes his intentions clear with a knife to Ricardo's ribs. The right half of the boy's face sags an inch below the left, and his eyelids are purplish and sickly looking. The newspapers have been reporting problems with marauding gangs in the capital. Ricardo looks around to see if anyone else is lurking nearby but the two of them are alone.

"What's your name?" Ricardo asks. "I'll give you my money but I need to know your name."

The boy stares at him like he's crazy. In answer, he pushes the blade through the poet's guayabera, breaking the skin. The pain chimes like a bell. Ricardo longs to touch the blood blossoming on his shirt but forces his eyes to stay on the thief's. He can't believe that this is how his life will end. Knifed by some punk for the twenty dollars in his pocket.

"Henry," the boy blurts out. "My name's Henry."

"Here you go, Henry." Ricardo gingerly reaches for his wallet. "Won't you regret this on your deathbed?" A long list of writers who suffered majestic injuries parades through Ricardo's head.

"What the fuck are you talking about?" Henry pushes the blade in another quarter inch, fusing them closer.

"Are you Catholic?" Ricardo gasps. He pictures himself as

Saint Sebastian; the boy's knife as an arrow, tipped with anesthetic.

"My brother's a priest," Henry boasts.

"I don't believe you."

"It's true. He says the five o'clock mass at Saint Regina's."

A bus squeals around the corner. The dank smell of the brick wall is overpowering. Ricardo thinks about his wife and Isabel forty yards away in the hotel. If he dies, Sarah might grieve for him by baking a big batch of éclairs or petit fours. But Isabel won't know what she's missed. He'd be gone, like he was gone for Barbarita.

"It's not so easy to kill a man," Ricardo whispers. "When I was a kid, it took two men and an ax to murder my father."

"What did he do?"

"He was a policeman in Cuba forty-five years ago. That didn't make him too popular."

Ricardo could tell Henry many things about his father. That he'd believed in the salutatory effects of enemas and submitted his family to them every Sunday before church. That he'd painted watercolors on those same Sunday afternoons. Years later, Mami showed Ricardo the cache of his father's watercolors that she kept stored in a cardboard trunk: portraits of street urchins and fishermen; one of Ricardo as an infant, with strikingly pink thighs; a series of disturbing self-portraits. Ricardo's ex-wife, Estrella, was also a painter. She used to say that portraiture was nothing more than a desperate attempt to evade oblivion.

"My father was a painter, too," Ricardo continues. "He would've wanted to paint you."

"Me? Why?"

"Because of your face."

"Shit," the boy says, his jaw muscles tightening. Perhaps the one who'd suffer most over his death, Ricardo thinks, is this boy with the crooked face.

There's an explosion in the distance, the sound of sirens. People run past the alley, shoes clattering.

"I want to live," Ricardo pleads quietly.

Without a word, Henry pulls out the knife with a shaky hand and slips away.

The News

From Radio El Pueblo

Demonstrators marched outside the National Palace today, demanding an immediate halt to foreign adoptions. The protesters charge that indigenous women are being targeted as baby breeders for the rich. "Our wombs are being used as factories," says María Ruíz Solano of Protect Our Wombs (POW). The women carried placards, shouting: "Don't Sell Our Future!" and "Our Babies Are Not Exports!"

"This is utter nonsense," countered Gertrudis Stüber, the country's top international adoption lawyer. "We're saving poor, unwanted children from destitution and giving them a chance for a more promising future."

The protests come in the wake of a notorious incident in August when a Japanese couple was beaten to death in the Highlands for photographing children. According to eyewitnesses, the campesinos believed that the tourists were planning to kidnap the children and harvest their organs for transplants abroad.

From an editorial in *El Observador*

With elections less than a week away, the presidential race is shaping up to be nothing more than a tragic recycling of previous campaigns. The list of promises is long but specific plans are nonexistent. Only one party has integrated the 1996 peace accords into its proposed platform. The preferred style is messianic, led by the ex-dictator who, recent polls show, is tied for second place . . .

From the Weather Channel

Tropical storm Odette has been upgraded to hurricane status as it picks up strength through the Lesser Antilles. Seventeen inches of rain have fallen there in the last twenty-four hours, turning coastal Grenada, Barbados, St. Lucia, and Martinique into virtual swamplands. The hurricane is expected to reach the Dominican Republic early Thursday.

From *Noticias Siete*

An explosion rocked the Hotel Encanto this afternoon, killing two German tourists and a U.S. embassy official. No one has claimed responsibility for the blast but authorities suspect that leftist terrorists are to blame. Investigators found the remains of a cheap wristwatch they believe contained sufficient cordite to detonate the blast. The U.S. embassy issued a statement regretting the death of their visa officer, twenty-eight-year-old Robert Minor, who was transferred to the capital only two weeks ago . . .

From *The Lupe Galeano Show*

Lupe Galeano: There are so many delicious rumors about you, Suki, almost too naughty to recount on the air. Let's review a few of the tamer ones: that you drink egg-yolk-and-beef's-blood shakes for breakfast; that you ingest whale pheromones in order to dominate the bulls; that your father was a tango dancer who taught you everything you know. Are any of these true?

Suki Palacios (*laughing*): Yes, they're all true, Lupe, every word. Especially the one about the whale pheromones.

L.G.: I can see you're not averse to a touch of scandalous publicity, eh? Aren't you afraid your fans will turn on you if you go too far?

S.P.: My fans are my fans because I go too far. I live too close to death to avoid life.

L.G.: So you dare to do what the rest of us only dream about?

S.P. (*wryly*): I didn't know you harbored ambitions of entering the ring yourself.

L.G.: Oh, dear no! Facing an angry, snorting mass of muscle intent on my destruction is not my idea of fun!

S.P.: Well, what else is there to do around here on a Sunday afternoon?

CHAPTER THREE

*An anatomy lesson • The ex-guerrilla considers
the relative merits of arsenic • A communiqué from Korea •
The colonel receives an unexpected chocolate cake • The news*

TUESDAY

Soon I will know who I am.

   —Jorge Luís Borges

Room 719

The lady matador enjoys a breakfast of melon and green tea while studying her anatomy book. She's focused this morning on the wrist joint and its radio-carpal wonders. The wrist is essential to what's most beautiful in the ring—the flourishes of the cape; the final, unhesitating thrust of the sword. Male matadors frequently neglect the wrist because they already walk a tenuous line appearing publicly in pink stockings and a suit of lights. Suki has no such qualms. Her goal is simple: to employ her wrists to turn the bulls so short they fall to their knees.

La matadora divides her time between the days she fights the bulls and the days she doesn't. She's agreed to do another exhibition fight tomorrow, so today she must rest, pamper herself, conserve her strength. Suki is eager to try a few new moves or, rather, moves so old they'll seem new again. Recently, she's been analyzing film clips of the fabled Joselito, the Spanish bullfighter who was a contemporary of her grandfather Ramón. At the height of his career, Joselito had no peers. Only true aficionados knew how dangerously he worked. Nobody today celebrates the great Spanish matadors of the Golden Age. In those days, a top bullfighter earned more in one afternoon than Babe Ruth did all year long.

Suki pours herself another cup of tea. She plucks a melon seed off her tongue and settles on the floor to stretch. The carpet scratches her legs but she spreads her thighs wide and leans forward, popping her hip joints. Then she lies flat on her back and extends her arms overhead. Last night, she dreamed that her mother was climbing a tree with a crossbow over her shoulder. Up, up, up her mother climbed until she was no more than a speck on the highest limb. Above her, an intricately embroidered kimono unraveled in the sky. She woke up lonelier than when she'd gone to bed.

Suki ultimately plans on becoming an orthopedist and finding a cure for what killed her mother. When Mamá was sick, Suki cloaked her in sunny, quilted fabrics to bulk up her diminishing frame, lessen her insignificance. The Santa Anas were blowing hard the last weekend her mother was alive. Fires burned in the hills. At night, the moon looked red and shrouded, reflecting the destruction. Mamá announced that she wanted to die in Yokohama but there wasn't enough time or money to arrange the trip.

Afterward, Papi had her buried in a weedy Catholic cemetery in Boyle Heights.

The lady matador crosses one knee over the other and drops her legs into a spinal twist. She pictures herself as a medical school skeleton, loosening each one of her thirty-three vertebrae. Suki remembers one of the cadavers she'd carved up in anatomy class: a hooker, judging from the condition of her reproductive organs. What killed her, though, wasn't the unchecked syphilis or gonorrhea but an ax blow to the skull.

Many specialties intrigued Suki in medical school: pulmonology, oncology, anesthesiology. Only podiatry didn't interest her. Suki is particular about feet. If she doesn't like a man's feet, she won't sleep with him. She's made last-minute reversals on this alone. Yesterday's waiter had excellent feet: proportionate toes, a good arch, thick metatarsal padding, shapely heels. Yes, it proved to be a highly satisfactory afternoon.

The phone rings and Suki hesitates before answering. She doesn't like to be disturbed on the day before a fight.

"Those other *matadoras* will be crying for mercy by the time you get through with them!" Her father's voice crackles exuberantly through the receiver.

"Hey, Dad. How are you?"

"*Ay,* I can't twist like I used to with these arthritic knees. And now they want to replace my hip!" He lowers his voice. "Have you found another manager yet?"

"No way."

"Because you just say the word and I'll return."

"No one will ever take your place."

"*Gracias, hija.*"

"So are you really coming down for the fight?" Suki loves her father but he can be more of a handful than the bulls.

"I'm taking the bus."

"From Veracruz? Are you crazy?"

"An express will get me there in twelve hours." Her father sounds hurt but he tries to hide it by changing the subject. "How's your sword work?"

"You saw the fight in Zacatecas?" Suki's sword handle broke at the crucial moment and she left the ring amid a storm of seat cushions.

"That's why I'm asking."

"I've had the hilt reforged. And I'm working on strengthening my wrists."

"One can't forget the wrists." He pauses, whispering dramatically. "I've heard Paloma is training with a boxing champ."

"That shouldn't be much use unless the bulls decide to charge on their hind legs."

"Pay attention to me, Suki. It's no joking matter. She's become like that . . . that . . . Muhammad Ali."

The morning light lingers on her sheathed sword.

"Look, Dad, it's not a dance competition. Besides, you know how nuts she is. Remember the time you caught her injecting that bull with Valium?"

"I could've used a little myself after that!"

"I've been concentrating on watching old footage of Joselito. He didn't fake anything. In the end, I have to believe my performance will speak for itself."

"*Bueno,* you can't go wrong learning from the classics." Papi's mood grows more buoyant. "But it *is* a lot like dancing, you know: supple hips, supple wrists, supple hips, supple wrists, supple—"

"Are you coming alone?" Suki interrupts, flexing her calf muscles. She reminds herself to order another ripe pear from room service.

"I think you might like my girlfriend this time. She's, eh, more mature than the last one."

"The last one was seventeen!"

"Forgive an old man his follies."

"And this one?"

"Let's say she's old enough to be your—"

"Don't say 'mother.'"

"Not exactly."

"Grandmother?"

"Try again."

"For God's sake, just tell me."

"She's seventy-six, a young seventy-six. Looks more like seventy-two. A devotee of Our Lady of the Flattering Light. And she's terrified to fly."

Suki laughs in spite of herself. "How's her eyesight?"

"Like a bull's." Her father chuckles. "I want you to be nice to her, *hija*."

"All bets are off since you surpassed the fifty-girlfriend mark."

"Has it been that many? *Ay*, who's keeping count?"

"I am. This is bachelorette number fifty-two."

"*Sí*, but it's been ten years since your mother died. Fourteen since we divorced."

"Do the math, Dad."

"Will we get a chance to dance together?"

"Uh—"

"A nice cha-cha-cha?"

As a child, Suki spent hours at her father's studio in East L.A.

imitating his students' dance steps. When his tape deck broke, Suki kept the rhythm for him on the clave. By the time her parents divorced, she was his star pupil. That same spring, Papi entered her in a national dance competition for children but Suki placed only fifth. Soon afterward, her father moved back to Veracruz. It was during her summer vacations there that she grew interested in fighting bulls.

"So she's loaded?" Suki persists.

"A spirited mambo perhaps? Something by Pérez Prado?"

"Aren't you getting too old to be a gigolo?"

"*Mi amor,* it's not a question of age!"

"Since when do you need a woman to pay your bills?"

Papi has only a few students at his dance school in Veracruz. Most everyone there can already dance and those who can't wouldn't dream of paying to learn. Papi's clients are largely tourists. He hires himself out as a dance partner, too—for the lonely, foreign women.

"That's easy for you to say, my little heiress. An old-fashioned *danzón,* that's what we should do!"

No one could dispute that Rogelio Palacios's *danzón* is a thing of beauty. If a lion could dance, he would look like the regal Rogelio.

"Whatever you want." Suki is exasperated but she won't make much headway over the phone. Outside her window, there is an eruption of crows from a pomegranate tree.

"Don't disappoint me!" he begs.

"See you soon, Dad."

"Your name is a silver bell in my heart!"

Suki finishes her stretching exercises and runs a hot bath. She orders a bowl of lemons from room service. She'll drop these, half smashed, into the water to release their oils. Her mother was fond of lemons. When Mamá's bones began disintegrating, she'd heat up fish sticks for dinner almost every night and serve sliced lemons on the side. To heal a wound, Suki thinks, one must reopen it again and again.

Garden Restaurant

The adoptive mothers are gathered in the garden restaurant for their midmorning ritual. This is Aura's least favorite part of the day. She'd rather clean toilets, fend off advances from men twice her age, do anything besides deal with these demanding, entitled women. The mothers come to show off their babies and commiserate over the maddening pace of the local bureaucracy. It's not enough that Aura waits on them hand and foot. They also expect her to coo over and dandle their babies (it's become something of a competitive sport), warm up their formula, dispense impracticable advice. All this they want with unfailing solicitude. It's no use telling them that she's inexperienced with children, that she was the youngest in her family and never had a child of her own.

The ex-guerrilla brings over a platter of *guayaba* pastries and a fresh pot of coffee. She wonders if these women would have anything in common back home. Only their trophy children, sought out in the tropics, keep them talking. Most of them have been at the hotel for a month or more waiting for their adoption papers to come through. Without their business, the hotel would be half empty. Years of civil war have kept the tourists away, probably for good.

A lesbian couple from San Francisco holds court with their

new son, Eduardo Wolf. They demonstrate to the other mothers how to massage a fussy baby's adrenal glands, something they learned in a self-help group. Every child present is impeccably dressed except for the jittery new mother's, who is spattered with mashed banana. The baby girl's hair sticks up in every direction and her fingernails are dirty. The mother, Sarah Morán, bolts back double espressos like shots of whiskey. She describes the city's architecture as "half-breed."

Aura feels sorriest for the babies of the fundamentalist Christian mothers. She imagines the children years from now in starched dresses and miniature suits, forced to sit still in church, bend to rituals not their own. Who of them will get to savor a homemade tortilla, hot from the grill? Aura learned how to pat the dough to just the right thickness without overworking it. She was six the first time she made tortillas, and badly burned her fingertips. Afterward she climbed their lime tree with her salted hand (salt drew out the heat, Mamá said) and reached for the soothing stars.

Nothing in her life, Aura thinks, has turned out the way it should. Mamá taught her everything she needed to know to become a good wife and mother: how to properly sweep a dirt floor, kill a chicken, mend a sleeve, embroider a *huipil*. But none of this has done her any good. She's neither a wife nor a mother and, it seems to Aura, hardly a woman. When men react to her, Aura ignores them, if she bothers to notice them at all. She's no more than a sturdy pitcher: practical and useful, not intended for display.

"Aren't these delicious?" Someone passes around the *guayaba* pastries. "I've gained ten pounds from these things since I got here."

The messy baby's mother sniffs at the pastries and twists a napkin in her lap. The conversation turns to the explosion at the Hotel Encanto, two blocks away (the women shudder at the news), upcoming doctor visits (Dr. Antonio Barillas is considered the best pediatrician in town), the pros and cons of local formula (good only for transitioning to American brands is the consensus), the coming hurricane (it's flooding everything in its path), the number of military men at the hotel (alarming for most; enticing to a few), and the gossip surrounding the lady matador.

"Everyone is drooling over her," reports Brooke, a horse trainer from New Jersey who bounces a flat-headed boy on her knee.

"I hear she has sex with a different man every night," whispers the busybody interior designer from Dallas. "The bellman told me."

"Lucky her," one of the lesbians blurts out, and everyone laughs.

Aura has seen the lady matador up close, when she delivered an imported pear to her room on Sunday. *La matadora* gives the impression of existing beyond gender—a new, more sublime species. She was very picky about how the pear should be served—on white china, with a full set of silverware and a crystal goblet of mineral water. She gave the ex-guerrilla a five-dollar tip.

When the mothers' tea is done, Aura hauls a sack of sugar from the stockroom and gathers more pepper, hot sauce, and cream for her station. There's a cage of ragged turkeys in the kitchen dolefully destined for mole sauce. Glassy-eyed cod are piled high on the chopping block. If she's lucky, the colonel will have lunch here today. She needs to get a better look at him, assess his strengths and weaknesses. Are his reflexes quick? What kind of gun does he carry? How suspicious is he?

Last night's explosion at the Hotel Encanto has everyone on edge. The busboys and kitchen staff are jumpy—dropping linen, serving spoons, a jar of Spanish olives. The chef is in the foulest mood imaginable, banging pots and pans, a twelve on a scale of ten. Aura ignores them and continues stocking her station. She wonders who planted the bomb. All sorts of clandestine groups have sprung up since the peace accords but nothing has changed. A generation of civil war, and for what? To fill the history books with lies? Only *el pueblo* knows the truth of what they've suffered.

Aura barely slept last night, trying to decide what to do. Certainly Julio can't expect her to gun down the colonel over a plate of huevos rancheros. She could kill him all right (she's imagined it a thousand times) but it has to be foolproof. If she gets caught, or her attack fails, the colonel wins. Again. Aura doesn't want to risk her life for his anymore.

Maybe she could don a wig and high heels to seduce the colonel. The thought sickens her. *Ay,* she's no voluptuary. Even younger and more beautiful, she wasn't cut out to be a seductress. Sometimes she forgets she has a body at all. A number of female guerrillas managed to dispatch their share of military men in bed but Aura bowed out of those assignments.

Her pistol is rusty and unreliable. Strangling would be quieter but next to impossible with someone as muscular as the colonel. Not that she wouldn't relish seeing him slumped lifelessly against a length of telephone cord. A hatchet blow would do the trick. Or she could surprise him with something blunt: a rock, a hammer, a baseball bat.

A letter arrived from Cristina this morning, anticipating Aura's crisis: *You will be tempted by the Devil himself but do not succumb to his solicitations or be damned to the everlasting flames beseech our Savior for guidance dearest Sister you know I cherish you forever Amen.* Cristina takes credit for Aura leaving the jungle but her prayers had nothing to do with it. Aura deserted the rebels because she was disgusted with endangering the lives of the very campesinos she was supposed to be protecting.

Aura sighs as she refills the pepper shakers. Whole centuries could pass before history itself brings the country's criminals to justice. What wouldn't she give to have Bruce Lee's skills for a day. There was a time when she collected statistics on Lee's physical feats: 250 thumb push-ups, 75 one-armed chin-ups, punching a 300-pound sandbag to the ceiling twice in a row. Aura is discouraged by her limitations. For Lee, there was no worthier pursuit than avenging the death of innocents. He made killing seem like a righteous act. But Aura no longer sees the world so starkly.

"Everything okay?" the bartender asks, adjusting his bow tie. Miguel likes to make glasses sing by spit-rubbing their rims with his finger.

"I'm a little tired." Aura tries to smile. He could never guess at the storm in her brain.

"Come, I want to show you something." Miguel steers her toward the caged parrots, draped with tablecloths and lined up under the pergolas for their siesta. "I've taught Osvaldo something new."

With a flourish, he removes a checkered cloth and the spasmodic parrot comes to life. Miguel offers it a handful of mixed nuts from his stash at the bar. Osvaldo fluffs his feathers, then screaks: *Without your gaze my heart is the enemy in my chest! More cashews, amigo!*

Aura bursts out laughing. "I see he's moving from revolution to love."

"I suppose you could say that." The bartender shifts from one foot to the other.

Aura suspects that Miguel likes her but she couldn't be less interested. He could be Che Guevara incarnated and she wouldn't be interested. Well, maybe she'd make an exception for Che. But she has too much on her mind as it is. Aura feels Miguel's stare as she returns to the kitchen.

At the entrance to the supply closet, an insect strip congested with desiccated flies skims her shoulder. She inspects the stockroom, where a carton of the strips sits on a shelf next to the rat poison. Aura reads the ingredients: a long list of chemicals she can't pronounce, except for one—arsenic.

Hotel Bar

Won Kim orders a whole roast chicken at the hotel bar. No side dishes or anything to drink. Just the chicken and an ashtray. Won Kim sits in a corner of the lobby bar, at a table smaller than his oversized plate. The chicken is the first thing he has eaten all day. He examines the density of the dark meat, its rubbery tendrils of veins, then abruptly tears a hunk of white meat from the breast bone. Won Kim eats and smokes, smokes and eats until there is nothing left of the chicken except a swatch of pimply, undercooked skin.

There are many things Won Kim must do today but only one thing he wants. Yesterday, his mistress refused to budge from the hotel and so his plans for their seaside excursion were ruined. Won Kim cannot deny that he was born unlucky. For the first three months of his life, he had white hair, like an old man, and was wrinkled all over. His relatives said he resembled the Asian elephants his mother had obsessively watched at the zoo. Baby Elephant, everyone called him, thinking him preternaturally wise. But that early promise came to naught.

At least he had managed to avoid consummate disgrace until now. Now his name is being dragged through the mud alongside the rest of the tropical dung. And there is no one he can blame for this treachery. Won Kim traces an absentminded thumb along his temple. It is only a matter of time before the scandal trickles back to his family.

He lights another cigarette, expelling the smoke from his lungs in one long breath. Won Kim could sit here and list his regrets over multiple cartons of cigarettes and still not be done. To begin with, he has never seen a whale. He has never slept with a woman he loves. Nor has he ever slept with a woman like *la matadora,* something he desperately wants but would be too afraid to do. Nobody has ever told him "I love you," not even his mother or sisters. He has never said "I love you" to anyone, although he has felt it twice, when he was young and collecting bugs.

Above all, Won Kim wanted to discover a new species of butterfly. He was first smitten the morning he saw a piece of bark fly away as a moth. How ingenious it was to disguise oneself so thoroughly. *He* was that moth, he decided, hiding inside a deceiving exterior. How else could he survive in his father's house? From that day forward, Won Kim spent every spare hour hiking in the mountains with a net and a magnifying glass.

By the time he was fifteen, he had one of the finest butterfly collections in the country. He corresponded with lepidopterists from around the world and once, shyly, displayed his most prized specimens before an entomology class at the University of Seoul. Under pressure from his father, Won Kim donated his butterflies to the capital's nascent science museum, where they eventually, neglectfully, turned to dust. Partly out of mourning, partly out of revenge, Won Kim took to occasional petty thievery (mostly hammers and screwdrivers, tools that could both build and destroy) and reading natural history books. Once he came across a passing reference to butterflies in a collection of poetry and copied it down.

And there will fly into the room
A colored butterfly in silk
To flutter, rustle and pit-pat
on the blue ceiling . . .

A bellboy delivers a telegram to Won Kim at the bar. He tips the boy and carefully opens the envelope. The message is from his mother, pleading with him (again) to return home to Seoul and bury her like a proper son. *I cannot die in peace with you so far away.* Won Kim folds the telegram, his face burning with shame.

"I want your biggest steak!" he shouts to the bartender.

Other customers turn to look at him but Won Kim no longer cares what anyone thinks. Let them speculate about his transgressions. Let them revel in his sins. Let them strip him bare and see him for who he is. At the bar, Won Kim recognizes the barrel-chested colonel but cannot remember his name.

The television drones on behind the mahogany bar and Won Kim tries to distract himself with the weather report. A hurricane, apparently, is churning its way toward their shores. If only he could be swept away by its purging winds. How he would relish tumbling through the air with the pelicans and dusky fish, their gills opened and red as new wounds. Just as a report begins on the lady matador, the same colonel gruffly orders the TV turned off.

Won Kim cuts his rare steak. It is juicy and delicious, better than the chicken, but he cannot force himself to eat more than one bite. His stomach flip-flops and the burning in his lungs spikes down to his knees. He smokes another cigarette to settle his nerves. Then he pays for his food with two twenty-dollar bills and heads upstairs to his mistress.

Berta opens the door to their honeymoon suite wearing a crimson gown with old-fashioned bustles and crinoline. Atop her head sits a powdered wig piled high with ringlets. A table with white linen is set with freshly peeled fruit.

"Do you like it?" she asks demurely, spreading her arms.

Won Kim smiles. He wants nothing to be upsetting his mistress from her genial mood. If dressing up like an eighteenth-century harlot makes her happy, so be it.

He takes Berta's hands and brings them to his lips. Her usual milky scent is replaced by something complexly floral. He looks down at her belly, well concealed under fathoms of imported silk. The fabric looks French and frightfully expensive. Won Kim prays that she did not have this outfit custom made.

Berta's jaw slides forward, as if suddenly unhinged. She points a trembling finger at the telephone on the nightstand. "Can you hear it?"

Won Kim strokes her hands and wrists. He does not want her agitated.

"Yes, I can. Of course I can. You are my sweet girl." Her jaw shifts back into place, and he is reassured. "Now close your eyes and open your mouth."

Her face is rouged and powdered, her eyelashes thickened with mascara. Her lips part and the stark pinkness of her tongue astonishes him. Won Kim reaches into his pocket and deposits a mint on the tip of her tongue.

"You can open them now." He touches a loose tendril of her wig, stiff as straw.

Berta sucks hard on the mint until it is gone, then reaches for Won Kim. Roughly, she removes his jacket and pulls off his belt with sure fingers. Won Kim feels himself stirring. *Don't think, don't think at all.* His mistress leans forward, presses her minty lips to his, and tugs off his pants. She moves down his legs, massaging him everywhere, slips a finger between his buttocks. Won Kim is electrified. Then Berta pushes aside her tide of rustling silk and bends over the edge of the bed, naked with grace and open for him. In a flash of guilt, Won Kim thinks: *I have wronged you for the rest of your life.*

Balcony

The colonel pulls open the French doors to his balcony and looks out over the ancient banyans. The unseasonable morning haze nearly sends him back to his air-conditioned room. Martín surveys the perimeters of the garden, cranes his neck up to the hotel's higher floors—then beyond, to the skies. Not even the cumulus clouds escape his inspection. The Miraflor is a fortress, Martín reminds himself. Only the restaurant ten floors below, with its pink-and-white uniformed waitresses and—the colonel whiffs the air—its platters of fried eggs and ham, is vulnerable. The hotel is pink and white, too: white on the outside and pink on the inside, like a conch, or a gringa's pussy.

Martín settles onto the floral cushion of a wicker chair with a stack of newspapers. He's eager to read any reports about his speech Sunday night. Three of the eight presidential candidates were in attendance, including the ex-dictator, who incited a noisy group of protesters outside the hotel. Martín's speech drew prolonged applause and numerous hearty encomiums. Only the ex-dictator pulled the colonel aside and, with a perfectly proportioned smile, advised: "Words may go far, young man, but bullets go farther." That is to say, violence is the most eloquent language of all.

The colonel scours the English-language daily first but there's nothing about his speech, only an inside spread on the Argentine military delegation. The paper is terribly written and ill-informed, but it's the one the U.S. embassy relies on most. When Martín went to train with the Yankees in Georgia, he applied himself day and night to learning English, the southern kind, with vowels so elastic they felt like rubber bands in his mouth. In no time, he was translating the drill sergeants' curses for the other Spanish-speaking recruits. The food in the mess halls, swimming in grease, helped loosen his tongue. He swore he sweated Crisco the whole summer long.

A front-page piece in *El Nuevo Tiempo* reports on the threat of a massive workers' strike. No surprise there. The unions have been warning of this for months. There's a long article on Congress's attempt to block international adoptions and an exposé on a Korean maquiladora. Buried on page twenty-six is a two-inch note on his speech. It misquotes him twice—*hijos de puta*—but no real damage is done. Today's editorial in *El Observador* is scathing, accusing the army (yet again) of whitewashing the "genocide." No mention of him there, at least.

A flock of pigeons flies in a wide ellipse over the garden. The colonel rolls his shoulders—they're stiff from his morning workout. He watches the birds skim the tops of the palms. The faint clink of silverware drifts up to him from the garden restaurant. A shapely waitress refills water glasses from a silver pitcher; another straightens the linen. He spots the heliotrope, flagrant at the edge of a flower bed. A red-shouldered blackbird comes out of nowhere and lands on his balcony railing. It stares at him, unblinking as a camera. Martín shoos it away.

Back in his room, the colonel pours himself a morning scotch from the minibar. He's ill at ease but can't say why. Talismans of his existence are scattered on the dresser: cufflinks, gold watch, ribbed socks rolled up just so. Martín tries to picture himself when he was someone else: a boy who loved adventure books; a boy whose mother paid a healer to protect him from the river ghost; a boy whose father, a *ladino,* wore linen suits and won seven mayoral elections in a row (he always ran unopposed); a boy afraid of swimming who learned to swim; a boy afraid to kill who learned to kill.

Martín spies the lady matador strolling by herself in the garden. Perhaps it's she who's causing his uneasiness. He wants to call out to her, toss her the rosebud from his bedside vase. She's wearing a tiger-striped bodysuit that makes her look like the beast itself, all lithesome power. The colonel half expects her to emerge from the foliage with a dead zebra between her teeth.

There's a knock at the door and a skeletal bellboy delivers a letter to him on a silver tray. The boy reminds him of his older brother, Alfredo, all skin and bones, who disappeared when he was fourteen. Martín remembers the last time he saw Alfredo, behind the sacristy. A revered old priest, Padre Bonifacio, was licking, delicately as a preening cat, his altar boy brother's penis.

The envelope is cream-colored, addressed to the colonel in a flourish of lavender ink. It smells subtly of jasmine. The note is unsigned, succinct: *My dearest colonel, Soon you will be mine . . .* Martín turns and searches for the lady matador in the garden but there's only that damn parrot screeching more revolutionary crap.

At army headquarters downtown, rumors are circulating that more bombs will go off tonight. Intelligence agents are zeroing in on terrorist cells with tentacles in the city's hotel unions. The colonel's informants are warning of more bloodshed this week, disruptions on a scale to make the world take notice. The conference is precisely the sort of opportunity the leftists are looking for. Martín switches on three televisions, preset to the major news stations, then flips on a staticky radio.

Martín decides to spend a couple of hours in his office before returning to the hotel for the afternoon seminars. He picks up his letter opener, fashioned after a sixteenth-century Spanish sword. He inherited the opener from his father, along with his immodest desk, his meager library, and replicas of the *Niña,* the *Pinta,* and the *Santa María.* Severo Abel was shot dead behind this very desk twenty-three years ago. A dozen people saw the killers take off for the jungle on scooters, but nobody was arrested for his murder. Martín blames the leftists for this, for the desecration of Papá's tombstone years later. Only atheist scum could do what they did.

His secretary brings in the day's mail. There's a card from his ex-wife in Connecticut. Silvia writes to him at his office to keep their relations impersonal. News from her is never good and invariably includes a demand for money, unreasonable sums that presuppose Martín is stealing from the government, which he is not. He slips the tip of the sword under the back flap of the envelope and tears it open.

Two sentences in, the colonel roars: *¡Coñocarajohijadelagranputamadremaldita!* If that bitch thinks she can get away with this, she has sorely underestimated him. Remarrying? His sons up for adoption by some Yankee *pendejo* insurance executive? Is she out of her fucking mind? How dare she try to annul him from their lives! If she were standing in front of him, he'd aim between her eyes.

Martín tucks the letter inside his jacket pocket and stares at the row of televisions. Damn it, he can't afford to think about this right now. He turns up the volume on a feature about *la matadora*. A quick series of cuts shows her battling bulls in every major ring in Mexico. The interview with a top Spanish matador is venomous. *Women,* he says, *don't belong in the ring. Wherever Suki Palacios fights, I won't. Case closed.* The expression on the lady matador's face is unchanging—driven and humorless, as if to say: *Killing is a grim business.*

Late that night, the colonel spots Suki Palacios in the hotel discotheque wearing a neon green jumpsuit. She's alone, dancing on the coppery floor. No one dares get close to her. Martín takes inventory of those in her thrall: a dozen or so Latin American officers (four of them singled out in last year's Amnesty International war crimes report); four lawyers; one very drunk congressman; five call girls, one with stupendously large breasts; the cocktail waitress; two bartenders; and a beleaguered busboy.

Martín stares at *la matadora,* willing her to notice him, but she doesn't give him a second glance. He should go right up to her and ask for a dance but her mocking stance at the pool unnerved him. Before Martín can work up his courage, she vanishes like La Viciosa, his favorite comics superhero. She was a fantastic *amazona* who could turn herself into a cat with a double blink of her eyes. As a boy, Martín used to look for her in every stray cat in his village, convinced that she would reveal herself to him alone.

A pompous Argentine general calls the colonel over to their table. It's been a long day of meetings, arguments, accusations. Martín is in no mood for more. He orders a glass of French cognac, silently toasting the departed *matadora.* He dreamed of her last night, menacingly swirling her cape in the ring, sword held high for the kill; only he was the sad-eyed bull, his hump of neck muscle exposed in longing. When he woke up, his goddamn testicles were sore.

"So what do you hear about Cuba?" the general asks.

That's the question on everyone's mind these days. It's said that El Comandante is suffering from intestinal cancer. That his insomnia has gotten worse (he purportedly sleeps only two fitful hours a night). That he's relying on a Yoruban priestess named Mimi for political advice. The real question is this: How the hell has that posturing, good-for-nothing Communist managed to stay in power for almost half a century? Even his mortal enemies grudgingly admire him for that.

"Everyone in his family lives to a hundred," Martín says. "If those crazy exiles in Miami haven't been able to get rid of him, nobody can."

"We'd have run him out of Havana in two days," the Chilean major sneers. "Don't forget how we took care of Allende."

The Chilean irritates Martín, who's grown weary of blind certainties.

"Allende, Allende, I'm sick of hearing about Allende!" a Paraguayan officer shoots back, whiskey sloshing in his tumbler. "Without Uncle Sam, we'd all be behind bars."

"What the fuck is that supposed to mean?" a squat Bolivian lieutenant colonel growls. If you took the man out of his uniform he could double as an ape. He grabs a bowl of salted peanuts from the table and empties it into his mouth for emphasis.

The hookers are hovering like gadflies. The big-breasted woman—she introduces herself as Felicia—zeroes in on Martín. Earlier this year, her name was Natasha and she worked at Madam Rosa's. No, it wouldn't hurt to bed her again. Back when he was a new recruit, it was Russian roulette in the whorehouse every night. Every night someone got the transvestite but was too drunk or ashamed to tell.

The other men joke and negotiate around the colonel, trying not to appear too desperate. Only the Bolivian ape doesn't know the rules. He shouts at another hooker in a blond wig and stilettos, demanding that she service him for free. Back home, he insists, he never pays for whores. "Fuck off!" she says and moves toward the Chilean major, which infuriates the Bolivian even more.

Martín drinks one last cognac before calling it a night. Felicia whispers a torrid stream of enticements in his ear. "You're just my type, *Papito. Ay,* I bet you're hung, too. *Un caballo* in bed, no? Well, you won't be sorry, *mi amor.* I'll be your sweet fever, your fiery angel in the lonely night." Where the devil do these whores come up with this patter? The script is unerringly flattering and picturesque—and damned if it doesn't work every time.

The colonel secures his wallet and valuables in his room's safety deposit box. No use inviting temptation. He has a terrible habit (as his ex-wife repeatedly told him) of falling asleep right after sex. It got their honeymoon off to a bad start. Making love wasn't the problem—they were wonderfully compatible—but rather the ten minutes afterward, when he was supposed to stay awake and shower her with compliments.

Martín opens a window and waits for Felicia to bribe her way upstairs. He listens to a cricket singing its monotony in the garden. For a moment, he imagines the voice of the river ghost, rising from the trees and the cathedral and the blue-black volcanoes. It's a seductive voice, feminine, unthreatening. A knock on the door interrupts the colonel's reverie. A bellboy pushes a trolley with a chocolate cake into his room.

"I didn't order this," the colonel barks. Next to the cake is another cream-colored envelope. Martín tears it open. *Our time is growing closer.* Jesus fucking Christ. He examines the trolley from every angle. Nothing underneath it or attached to the wheels. No plates, no knives, no napkins or forks, either. Is he supposed to dive in face-first?

Just as Martin is about to send back the cake, Felicia peeks in the door and squeals: "*Ay, precioso,* how did you know I love chocolate?" She skims a manicured finger along the frosting studded with hazelnuts and smears it on her lips.

The colonel dismisses the bellboy without a tip. Martín looks at Felicia and thinks twice about kissing her. He can't brush off his suspicions. But she wastes no time and grabs a hunk of the cake, coating the deep canyon of her cleavage.

"Come and get it, *mi cielo*," she taunts, waggling her titanic breasts.

The colonel can't hold back any longer. He buries his face in their mountainous warmth and begins lapping up the chocolate. It's delicious, the best he's ever tasted. Then he sets to conquering Felicia's breasts one at a time, licking them methodically, in diminishing concentric circles toward her blooming brown nipples.

The News

From the Weather Channel

Hurricane Odette blasted the eastern coast of Cuba today, knocking down power lines and sweeping to sea a row of oceanside homes near the colonial city of Santiago. Flooding of two feet and higher is common throughout the region. El Comandante has issued a state of emergency and is distributing Chinese-made rowboats to area residents.

From Radio Cristiana

Radio Cristiana: Welcome, General. Now, you've promised to share with our devoted listeners an important revelation today.

General: I'm very glad to be here with you, Ronaldo. My news is rather, eh, personal in nature, although it has far-reaching public implications.

[*Exaggerated pause*]

Now I swear on my father's holy grave that this is absolutely true: the Lord has personally asked me to lead His flock to salvation and deliver us into the ranks of civilized nations. He told me that I should not shirk my responsibility to Him, or to our good people.

R.C.: How did the Lord communicate with you?

G: Through my canary.

R.C.: Your canary?

G: That's right, Ronaldo. Last Easter morning I was sitting on my patio enjoying my breakfast when, all of a sudden, I could understand everything Pequi was saying. One moment she was an ordinary canary; the next, a messenger from God.

R.C.: How extraordinary!

G: As we know, the Lord works in mysterious ways. Our mission is to follow Him, not question his methods . . .

From *Lo Último*

A Miami-bound airplane exploded over the Caribbean this afternoon, ninety minutes after taking off from the capital. Officials say they don't yet know the cause of the explosion but suspect leftist terrorists are responsible. Among those on board was Federico Ladrón-Benes, president of the Universal Fruit Company . . .

From *El Pajarito*

My dear listeners, you must learn to live without ice. Do not ingest it, or risk imperiling your kidneys. Remember this: peacocks wheel their tails in the heat. So cultivate your tolerance for the hottest days—or get a big Spanish fan. Today's lucky color is pink. Pink, pink, pink! Do not, under any circumstances, undertake a business project involving the number four. That's all for now, *queridos* . . .

From Channel 9's *Top of the News*

Nine people died in an early morning fire at the Happy Feet Nightclub when toxic fumes from the burning linoleum floor asphyxiated patrons. Overcrowding and inadequate escape routes turned the popular men's club into a death trap. Six of the nine victims were Korean citizens attending Happy Feet's renowned floor show. Swiss-born female impersonator La Petite Vixen was also among those who died in the blaze. Mayor Zúnigas has vowed to launch a thorough investigation into the cause of the fire and to tighten building codes in the capital.

CHAPTER FOUR

*Another proposal for the ex-guerrilla • The lawyer
drives her red sports car • An attempt on the colonel's life •
Protesters at* el coreano's *factory • The lady matador faces a
formidable bull • The poet begins a pantoum • The news*

WEDNESDAY

It is the rose of smoke,
the ash rose . . .

—Xavier Villaurrutía

Hotel Kitchen

Aura uncoils the rolls of flypaper and drops them, one by one, into the water. An hour's gentle boiling should yield a solution lethal enough to make the colonel's morning coffee his last. Aura stirs the pot with a wooden spoon. In another life, for another man, she might be cooking chicken soup, or a pot of salty black beans. Instead she's simmering a deadly brew, like a witch or a murderess, in the small hours of the night. The flypaper floats to the top of the bubbling broth. Aura holds the blanching strips underwater with her spoon, imagines them leaching their poison, the poison moistening the colonel's lips, his tongue, lining his gullet. She turns up the flame. How long will it take for his eyes to bulge, for his stomach to cramp? A man like him will know when his time has come. It's this knowledge that keeps her stirring.

Outside, the trees shiver in the downpour. Aura imagines an angel shaking a giant gourd in heaven, releasing billions of drops at once. She pictures this angel—rosy-cheeked with gilded wings, wearing something like a Communion dress—but not the God her sisters assure her is watching over them. If He does exist, then He must be on an extended vacation. The rain roars down harder. Aura endured many torrents like this in the jungle with only a scrap of plastic as a roof to keep her dry. Rainy nights were the most propitious for surprise attacks. The army patrols would be lazing in their barracks, playing cards and drinking beer, oblivious to the guerrillas circling outside.

Aura killed for the second time on a night like this—a boy, no older than fifteen, his face soft and plump as a girl's. She knew his first name, Ernesto, and that he was an informer who was endangering the lives of the guerrillas with his false reports. He squealed and shat like a piglet when Aura slit his throat from ear to ear. She didn't sleep for a month after she did it. No amount of washing removed the boy's stink from her skin. In fact, the stench intensified with every subsequent death.

The sound of a key in the lock freezes the ex-guerrilla in place. It's probably the security guards making a last obligatory round. She hopes that whoever it is will be satisfied with the locked door and move on. Aura dashes for the industrial refrigerator and pulls out a hunk of frozen meat—pork or beef, she isn't sure which. She could drop the meat in the pot and say she's preparing a stew for tomorrow's lunch, but it might reduce the arsenic's potency.

The door opens slowly, a chain of keys dangling from the lock. It's Miguel, the bartender from the garden restaurant.

"*Ay*, what a night," he sighs. He's sweaty and wild-haired.

"You scared the hell out of me." Aura is furious. "What are you doing here?"

"I've come to be your apprentice. I mean, accomplice." Miguel grins and this annoys her even more. He seems to have twice as many teeth as he should.

"I'm only making beef stew."

"With flypaper? Hmmm, that should be tasty."

"What do you want?" Aura fingers the butcher knife in her apron.

"We're more alike than you realize." He holds up both hands in surrender. "I'd appreciate it if you'd lose the knife, *compañera*."

Aura is surprised but not shocked. Nothing shocks her anymore.

"You were in the movement?"

"I still am," Miguel says, lowering his hands. "We've been planning this for months."

He pulls a sugar biscuit from his pocket and offers it to her. When she refuses, he nibbles on it like a rodent.

"Planning what?"

"Don't tell me you don't know." Miguel dusts the crumbs from his shirt.

"My reasons are personal."

"Perhaps we can help each other?"

"I have one debt to pay." Aura watches the pot of flypaper, which is boiling too vigorously, and lowers the flame. "Then I want to be done with this forever."

"I was fighting them when you were still a child. They're assassins, every last one."

"You don't have to tell me that."

"No, but I do need to remind you that it's not over yet."

"I don't want to know anything!" Aura is practically shouting.

"I can help you with the colonel." Miguel ignores her outburst. "If you return the favor, we'll secure your passage out of the country."

Aura slows her breathing like she used to in the jungle. Animals know how to ration their strength, blend in with their surroundings, feign death.

"You don't know anything about me," she whispers.

"I've been watching you for two years. I saw you spit on the general's pork chops."

"That means nothing—"

"I know about your brother. I know what they did to him."

In the library today, looking for information on arsenic, Aura came across an odd fact: a tribe in Papua New Guinea, when first shown the workings of a telegraph, fashioned a replica of it so they could talk with their dead.

Miguel pulls a plastic bag from his pocket filled with white powder. He holds it up to the light. "Arsenious oxide," he says. "Fatal in small quantities and mimics natural diseases: gastroenteritis, peripheral neuritis, dermatitis. The colonel, as I'm sure you know, suffers from ulcers. He's also prone to rashes and nerve degeneration in his left eye. I can give this to you but you need to help us first."

"I can't—"

"We have explosives, smaller than mouse traps. You could plant them in their rooms."

"Get someone in housekeeping to do it."

"There are spies in their ranks."

What have they ever talked about? Obnoxious guests. Kitchen gossip. Their favorite lines from Bruce Lee movies. Both agreed that Lee's all-time best line was "This time you're eating paper. The next time it's gonna be glass."

Miguel moves toward the pot of boiling flypaper and peers in. "I know that some wounds never heal," he says quietly.

Aura fights the urge to cry. For once she wants to be protected, to simply rest. "I have to think about it. I mean, no. I can't do it."

"We're counting on you." Miguel picks up the wooden spoon and stirs. "How much longer can we stand in line with tin cups?"

Aura looks at Miguel, as if for the first time. How stupid she was to ever think him ordinary.

La Hacienda

It's sunny out, the sky a uniform blue. The lawyer sits on her veranda finishing her morning coffee and biscotti. The gardeners methodically clip back the bougainvillea and mow the winter lawn. Tomorrow they'll prune the fig and avocado trees. Every summer, the groves yield enough fruit to bring in a tidy profit. Gertrudis watches a pair of lizards mate in a corner of her patio and thinks how silly human passion is next to this minimalism.

She tries to quiet her mind but it's hopeless, like balancing a beehive on top of her head. Gertrudis has made the necessary calls. Now it's only a matter of giving the calls sufficient time to take effect. She might've expected anything from her husband except pure treason. To her, an agreement is an agreement, no matter how unsentimentally it's made. Undoubtedly, written contracts are best but frequently impossible. When she'd been in grade school, Gertrudis had agreed to consider a lovelorn classmate's request for marriage but only if he put the proposal in writing. (She turned him down, nonetheless.)

The lawyer is surprised at how deceived she feels, at the wire of anxiety scraping her inside. After finishing her coffee, Gertrudis orders her car to be brought around—the German roadster she likes to drive herself. It's her custom to take it out for a spin on Sundays. Everywhere the lawyer goes—outfitted in driving gloves and goggles—people look on deferentially. Speculation will fly over the fact that she's driving her roadster on Wednesday. Let them talk. She's tired of caring.

Gertrudis settles behind the wheel and adjusts her side-view mirrors. Today she's a minefield of clarity, as if she can see in all directions at once. The barbed wire festooning her whitewashed walls looks funereal, like a widow's stiff lace. The wrought-iron gates of her mansion open smoothly. As she exits, Gertrudis nods to the lumpy security guard, midmeal in tamales and beans. She notes that the time is wrong on the bright face of the sentry's clock.

"Fix it," she orders him, tapping her watch. "It's three minutes slow."

The lawyer's first stop is seventy miles away, in the Highlands. She accelerates through her neighborhood, its avenues lined with thick-topped poplars. Every estate has its own security guards, armed with machine guns, like hers. It's not a choice but a necessity. Kidnapping has become a way of life. Gertrudis counts herself lucky. She has nothing criminals might ransom: no children, no pets, both parents long dead. The bank president down the street had his twin daughters kidnapped from their bedroom last Christmas. Only one survived. Evita, now sixteen, attends boarding school in Switzerland. And Señora Hochman's prize shih tzus were stolen over the summer. It cost her ten thousand dollars—negotiated down from double that—to get back those yapping balls of fluff.

A commotion is under way on the northwest road out of town, impeding traffic. Protesters are picketing Won Kim's Glorious Textiles factory, one of her chief suppliers. Gertrudis did business with Won Kim's father years ago, an ox of a man but not entirely without charm. Bon-hwa Kim had the audacity to try to seduce *la abogada*. Although his overtures fell flat, she rewarded his efforts with a sizable business account. Gertrudis cracks open her passenger window. The protesters are carrying signs and shouting slogans demanding more money, fewer hours, more benefits. Nothing new here. These jackals would eat everyone alive if they could. The lawyer honks as she passes, inhaling gasoline fumes. The protesters cheer, mistaking her impatience as a sign of solidarity. She doesn't have the time to disabuse them.

At last, Gertrudis speeds through the shantytowns skirting the tropical capital—shacks built from scraps of tin and wood, no plumbing to speak of, garbage collection nonexistent, electricity illegally siphoned off from power lines. Her competitors frequently scour these slums for pretty, underage girls whom they persuade to conceive children for the foreign adoption market. Gertrudis wouldn't sink so low. Her breeder mothers come strictly by recommendation and she makes certain that none of them is under eighteen. Many are married with children of their own. Their "work" provides extra income for their families.

On the twisting country roads, the lawyer lowers her windows and breathes in the fierce rush of scents: mango trees, goats, out-house stink. Cicadas hammer away in the grass and a shrunken woman sells iguanas from a basket on her hip. Gertrudis pictures purulent bats sleeping under the thatched roofs. The last forty miles takes her a half hour to drive.

Danila's parents are waiting for her in their just-swept yard. The two look withered as dried corn husks. The conversation is brief and unambiguous. The lawyer offers to buy the land they've been miserably working for years, put the deed in their name, throw in another acre for good measure. All this can be theirs on one condition: that Danila give up her baby for good. Gertrudis hands Danila's father a few bills as a down payment, and the deal is done.

The lawyer bought the downtown apartment building to house her breeder mothers. The building is old, the plumbing balky, but it's well situated and comfortable in every other respect. Her mothers lack for nothing here and are paid the highest rate in the industry. In return, Gertrudis expects their utter loyalty and discretion. Danila has failed her on both counts. It's a shame because her babies are the firm's most popular, snapped up within hours of their website postings. Danila's offspring have all been light-skinned and green-eyed like her, and they can pass for American.

Gertrudis knocks hard on the door before letting herself in with a master key.

"Hans warned me that you'd show up today," Danila says meekly from the crushed-velvet recliner. She's gained eighty-two pounds this pregnancy, far beyond what's healthy. Gertrudis credits the girl's indolence and the confines of an easy life. Danila blames it on the sacks of take-out Pollo Campero she's been putting on her expense account for months. The lawyer looks around the apartment, which is in disarray except for a well-dusted cabinet of porcelain figurines.

"Nobody dies of love or anguish, and neither will you," she says evenly. "But dying of hunger is another matter entirely." Gertrudis gazes at the mother's massive belly and lets that sink in for a moment. "You've had four children for me already, Danila. Each of them has been placed in a loving home in the United States. You're providing a service, a professional service, and you're paid accordingly. But this service comes with responsibilities."

"Yes, but Hans said—"

"Never mind what Señor Stüber said. Who employs you? Who pays for your medicine when you're sick? Who houses you and provides you with nutritious food? Not even the most generous husband will offer so much for so little."

Danila looks down at her swollen hands, adorned with cheap rings. Her back arches with defiance.

"Now you've broken my trust and that's not easily won again." Gertrudis leans toward Danila. The girl's skin is blotchy, her eyes pink-rimmed and rabbity.

"He promised to marry me!" she cries.

"There's only one problem with that. He's already married. To me." Gertrudis elongates the last vowel, then fixes her mouth in a straight line. "I've spoken to your parents—"

"*Mis padres, ¿por qué?*"

"—and we've come to an agreement regarding their future and yours. I expect you to abide by this agreement, or I can promise you that things will get unpleasant."

Danila pushes herself to standing. She lumbers to the kitchen and yanks out the cutlery drawer. Knives and forks clatter to the ground. She stares down at the mess of silverware, panting hard.

"There's no need for histrionics, Danila. It's all been arranged." Gertrudis leads her by the elbow back to the recliner. "Now you rest here. I don't want you worrying about another thing."

Late that night, Gertrudis examines herself in the full-length mirror of her boudoir. She's partial to her double-breasted cashmere suit, which showcases her narrow hips. She adds a matching fedora and crocodile pumps, then checks herself from behind. Perhaps she might pull off wearing a suit of lights like that lady matador. Gertrudis wonders how she'd fare in the ring. Certainly those bulls would be a cinch after two decades battling with Los Mohosos, her country's moldy politicians.

A frantic call from her secretary interrupts her musings.

"Repeat what you've said, very slowly," the lawyer instructs.

It's unusual for Gertrudis to leave the office early but tonight she had an important military banquet to attend at the Hotel Miraflor. She works hard to keep relations with the army exceedingly supple. Elva stayed behind to finalize preparations for the adopting couple from Tennessee. The banquet, predictably, turned out to be a colossal bore.

Hans stopped by the office just after nine o'clock, demanding Danila's files. When Elva said she'd have to check with *la doctora* first, he slapped her for disobeying him, then gagged her and tied her to a chair. As Elva helplessly watched, he opened the safe containing the lawyer's second set of records—the ones detailing the briberies, the baby buying, the tax evasion—and fled. The entire ordeal was over in fifteen minutes but it took her secretary three more hours to free herself.

"Where are you now?" Gertrudis is pacing. Her high heels leave an emphatic trail on her Himalayan rug.

"Aquí todavía."

"Has anyone seen you?"

"No, Doctora."

"Did my husband mention what he planned to do with the files?"

"He was taking them to the Justice Department," Elva says. "He said that by the time you found out, it'd be too late."

"Listen to me. Call the chauffeur and have him take you back to your apartment. Stay home tomorrow. Don't pick up the telephone. Don't answer the door unless it's me. Do you understand?"

"Sí, Doctora."

Gertrudis hangs up the telephone. On a hunch, she calls the airport and speaks to the night manager, Oskar Volk-Mendoza, an old German colony acquaintance. Oskar is paid well to overlook the municipal airport's scheduling irregularities.

"When did my husband's plane take off?" Gertrudis asks matter-of-factly.

"Two hours ago."

"Where to?"

"Miami."

"Gracias, Oskar." She makes a mental note to send him a thank-you bottle of schnapps.

It could be worse. The lawyer has many friends in Miami, including key contacts in the immigration service. Everything must be arranged behind closed doors, the scandal kept out of the media. Gertrudis steps out onto her balcony and surrenders to the aroma of her garden's faint ferment. She hears rats scuttling and scrapping in the bougainvillea. Nothing in this country ever changes, she thinks. It's always the rats that survive.

Room 1017

Damn, he shouldn't have drunk that cognac last night—and for what? To end up in the arms of that whore? Martín opens his eyes and looks across the bed. Felicia is gone. No sign of her clothes or purse. No light on in the bathroom, either, though the visible slice of pink tiles is painful to look at. Only the remnants of the chocolate cake and a wretched headache are left. Martín pushes himself up on one elbow and grows dizzy. His mouth is dry. A rash has broken out on his knees, no doubt from last night's exertions. His naked flesh feels soft and ripe, a victim's flesh. Sex is no longer the sweet medicine it once was.

The shower feels good, hard and metallic on his skin. Gradually, his vertigo recedes, but his stomach remains unsettled. Martín soaps himself up, lathering the hard lines of his body. When he's finally reunited with his sons, he'll make them work out with him every morning. All matter has the potential for fire. It's only a question of striking the match. Everything important in the world, the colonel knows, is determined by pressure. Too much pressure—or too little—yields disappointing results; just the right amount gets a man every damn thing he needs.

The doorbell rings as he's drying off. The colonel peers through the security peephole and answers the door with the towel wrapped around his waist.

"Who sent you?"

"Compliments of the hotel," the waitress says, crisp in her pink-and-white uniform. She carries a tray into his room and settles it on the desk. There's fresh-squeezed orange juice, a basket of breads and muffins, florets of butter, and a large pot of coffee. The napkin glares at him pinkly from the center of his white breakfast plate.

"What's your name?" the colonel demands, scratching his chest.

"Aura, sir." She's all professional attentiveness.

"Well, Aura, this is the third unasked-for delivery I've received since my arrival. Tell those *hijos de puta* in the kitchen that I want no more deliveries without my express approval. Is that clear?"

"Yes, sir. Would you like me to take away the trolley?" She indicates the ravaged chocolate cake.

"No, let it be."

"May I pour your coffee, sir?"

"Do I look like an invalid?" He flexes his pectorals, expecting to see her blush. But she doesn't. Martín grows still as a mineral. "Show me your identification."

"I beg your pardon?"

"Your identity card. Hotel employees are required to wear one at all times."

"Yes, of course." She isn't the least bit flustered by his request. This could mean two things: innocence, or excellent training.

Aura reaches into her apron and pulls out her laminated ID. The colonel examines it: Aura Estrada, thirty-six years old; born in

San Anselmo province; employed by the hotel since 2001. Martín and his troops spent months patrolling San Anselmo, flushing out the enemy, burning their *milpas* fields. A lot of women in those parts wore their hair braided down to their knees.

"What did you do during the war, Aura?"

"I don't know what you mean, sir."

"Where did your sympathies lie?"

"I was just working, sir. Same as everyone." Her gaze meets his. "Farming, factory work, whatever I could find. I was lucky to get this job."

"Do I look familiar to you?" Martín feels his cock stir beneath his towel. Even at his age, he can't control its predilections. Right now, it wants this ample-hipped waitress with the dimpled chin.

"No offense, sir, but I don't. Are you famous?"

The colonel bursts out laughing and his towel slips an inch. The path to military distinction is simple: destruction, and more destruction. "I guess you might say so. Tell me, Aura. Is there a patron saint of waitresses?"

"No, but there should be." It's her turn to smile. "Someone with a lot of patience."

The colonel looks at her hard, memorizing her face. "That will be all."

"May things go well for you, sir."

The four-star general from Paraguay drones on at the luncheon. Martín imagines him swelling like a hot-air balloon as a gaggle of street urchins take aim with their slingshots. He's heard it all before. The same rhetoric about weeding out the insurgents. The same prescriptions for monitoring university students. The same strategies for infiltrating the unions. The same tactics for funneling humanitarian aid back to the military.

"What's humane about giving money to criminals and moral derelicts who would do away with us altogether?" the general demands of the assembled. "A nation without a strong military is a nation ruled by chaos and lawlessness!"

The colonel pushes a greasy stuffed pepper around on his plate. His ulcer is acting up and his bad eye is twitching like a flea-bitten mutt. He has a sudden urge to bang a tambourine and watch everyone jump. It's impossible to concentrate. He must rescue his sons, take them away from their mother for good. Kidnapping is easy here but trickier in the United States. Perhaps he could invite the boys for Christmas, then refuse to send them back. By the time the legal maneuverings were done, his sons would be grown men at his side. They'd have no use for their mother or her sorry new husband.

Martín excuses himself, shaking hands with the Panamanian officers to his left and right. In the atrium, the twirling crystals from the fortune-teller's kiosk refract his face into a thousand pieces. What might she divine of his chances with *la matadora*? Martín stops at the florist and picks out a bouquet for Suki— roses mixed with tropical blooms. All hell breaks loose in the lobby when a stretch limousine disgorges another toreador. Martín catches a glimpse of her—freakily tall and with a nose like a hatchet. "La Paloma! La Paloma!" her fans shout out. But she's nothing like his lady matador.

"To the bullring," he orders the taxi driver, and they veer into noonday traffic.

As they're crawling past the cathedral, the colonel spots that pain-in-the-ass performance artist with her stinking bucket of blood. He should've done away with her years ago, when she was still a student. In that same instant, Martín glances in the tiny rearview mirror clipped to his sunglasses and spies two masked men on coughing blue scooters. Instinctively, he drops to the floor of the cab.

A burst of machine-gun fire shatters the taxi's back window, instantly killing the driver. His blood spatters the dashboard, the shuddering plastic statue of Saint Jerome. *¡Hijos de la gran puta!* Martín breathes hard. How easy it is to cut short a life. What once moved stops moving. It's as goddamn simple as that. He, at any rate, is still resoundingly alive. But the motherfuckers who did this won't be for long. As he crouches behind the passenger seat, the car crashes, as if suspended in time, onto the cathedral steps, scattering beggars and vendors and sending a spray of pink petals from the lady matador's bouquet shuddering through the air.

The Factory

The hot lights of the television cameras make everything look thickly painted: the hordes of protesters with their ragtag signs; the run-down school buses; the plantain bushes girding the entrance to the Glorious Textiles factory. In the middle of this chaos, the ex-dictator arrives in a cavalcade of sedans, megaphone in hand, seeking a photo opportunity. The reporters jostle around him, shouting questions. For all Won Kim knows, the tyrant paid for the protesters himself. In tough economic times, xenophobia is the cheapest form of publicity.

Won Kim wipes his face with a handkerchief. He is feverish and sweltering, though it is a mild autumn day. A dragonfly drones by, quivering and blue-eyed. Since the protesters arrived early this morning, Won Kim has not had a clear moment to think. His chest feels constricted, squeezed from within. He decides to forgo another cigarette for the moment. After five interviews in Spanish and Korean, he is confused and contradicting himself. His workers, too, are confused. Won Kim can only hope that this fiasco will blow over soon.

In his parking lot, vendors are hawking tamales and corn cakes, and a fish taco truck is doing brisk business. Won Kim hungrily sniffs the air. He is tempted to buy a couple of tacos himself—he has not eaten lunch in all the tumult—but if the television crews catch him snacking, he will appear too indifferent on the evening news. Of course, there is no real news here, only the wheels of the media grinding out more manure. Just then a minivan pulls up with a mariachi band wearing black velveteen breeches with gold trim. They strike up a lively ranchero, prompting the protesters to set down their signs and dance. Everything in this godforsaken country turns into a fiesta, Won Kim thinks irascibly.

When the protesters first appeared, Won Kim called the police but only one desultory officer showed up. As long as the demonstrators remain peaceful, the officer told him, he could not arrest anyone. Won Kim lost his patience: "So are you waiting for them to hang me from the acacia tree?"

Fifty yards away, the ex-dictator continues his speech directly under the GLORIOUS TEXTILES sign. ". . . And we won't permit our sovereign nation to suffer at the hands of those who don't have our best interests at heart. Because the proud souls of our people can't be broken by foreign devils with dubious agendas. We'll overcome them as we have overcome the exploitation and invasions of the past. Make no mistake about it. We will resist! We will fight! We will triumph!" He ends his diatribe by showering the protesters with coins. They squabble in the dust for the change like chickens. One woman with withered arms picks up two coins with her toes.

Won Kim's temples throb and his left elbow aches. A nice cup of rice wine would help him relax. But his doctor has forbidden him to drink as well as smoke—not to mention the ongoing ban on red meat. There is no abiding such misery. He might as well be dead. Won Kim glances around him. In spite of the music and dancing, the protesters are starting to look tired and their voices are growing hoarse. He gives them another hour before they pack up and go home. The more he thinks about it, the more Won Kim suspects Mr. Chong and Mr. Park, his fiercest competitors in the textiles market, of planting the sordid stories about him in the press.

Last night he was supposed to go to dinner with members of the Korean Manufacturers' Association and several investors from Seoul. To them, a good time is thusly proscribed: kilos of grilled meat, sky-priced whiskey, scantily clad women with mammoth breasts. It is an unvarying, one-size-fits-all junket. After yesterday's tumult, it was more than Won Kim could bear. Now he has learned that six of the men were killed in a fire at their favorite strip club. With any luck, he might have perished with them.

The day is bright as a madman. A red roadster coasts by on the highway, and the driver leans on her horn. Won Kim notices the license plate—ABOGADA. Where is Gertrudis Stüber driving off to on a Wednesday? Won Kim inherited her account from his father, who, he is certain, bedded the Teutonic lawyer. During his initial business call to her offices, Dr. Stüber looked Won Kim up and down with a gimlet eye and said: "You're not nearly as charming as your father."

As the ex-dictator departs in a flourish of meaningless pronouncements, another presidential candidate shows up for his share of the limelight. The reporters rush over to the reformist for a fresh comment on the "situation"—that being what to do about this unscrupulous *chinito* who is taking advantage of workers in their country. Won Kim wrings his hands, then looks down at his feet. He has been standing still for so long that a lizard has climbed onto his shoe, no doubt mistaking it for a rock. Several feet away, fire ants are devouring a dead tarantula.

The fast-talking reformist approaches Won Kim and peppers him with questions. "How long have you been in the country? How many employees do you have? What do you pay them hourly? Do you permit them sick days? What's your maternity policy? Do you speak fluent Spanish? Do you have a union here?" Won Kim does not answer him, only stares blankly at the politician in his fancy suit. It is made of fine worsted wool, too warm for today's weather. The man's mouth grows increasingly elastic, the lips stretched with hideous intent. Won Kim mutes the politician's words until they are unintelligible.

Instead he thinks about the sex he had with his mistress yesterday, pretending to be Louis XIV. "Call me the Sun King," he had pleaded, surprising himself. Whether it was the regal pretense, or the unfamiliarity of their half-naked bodies together, Won Kim felt a surge of hard lust run through him. Afterward they lay together amid the yards of expensive brocade and shared an unfiltered cigarette.

Won Kim's cell phone rings, startling him. "Hello, hello?" he answers, choking with hiccups. It is his oldest sister, Sook. She is sobbing and unable to form her words. Won Kim knows why she is calling. He lowers his shoulders, then rolls his neck from side to side, struggling for air. A stone weight crushes his chest. A hand bell in the mariachi band clangs loudly, echoing the bells in Korean funeral processions—its banners and life-sized dolls, its sea of white, coarse mourning cloth snaking toward church, toward eternity. His mother, permanent to him as the mountains, is dead.

He recalls her large-knuckled hands petting his own, the thumb-sized bald spots peeking through her feathery hair. Her pinched face begging him to refuse to go to the tropics, in spite of his father's request.

"There is much to discuss," his sister says shakily. "When can you return?"

Won Kim hangs up on her. Later, he will blame it on a bad connection. He walks behind the textiles factory into a tangle of vines. Once it had been a garden, now fallen into disarray. The air around him darkens. Beetles move furtively in the underbrush. A heavy languor invades his bones. He searches the bushes for a stray butterfly or moth, but winter has taken hold. Won Kim pictures clouds of butterflies surrounding him, leaking their colors into the moist air. His mother is among them, drifting lightly on a breeze and wearing her childhood face.

A bird he does not recognize circles over the wild grapefruit tree. Won Kim listens to its song, trying to decipher a message from the dead. *Fuiii, fuiii,* it calls, *fuiii, fuiii.* He found unspeakable things behind his factory during the war. The severed head of a curly-haired boy, bruised and swollen as a melon. A naked woman's torso missing all four limbs. What Won Kim would give to be a child again, thinking only a child's thoughts in the deep fir forests of home. He hears the hollow sound of fruit snapping from the tree and tries to control his grief, but he cannot. Won Kim falls to his knees, cradling his head, and cries out for his mother.

The Bullring

The lady matador chooses her royal blue *traje de luz* for today's fight. It's her oldest suit, and her luckiest. As she dresses meticulously—pink stockings first—she ticks off the cities in which she's gloriously slain bulls while sheathed in the suit's iridescence: Oaxaca, Juárez, Guerrero, Jalisco, Veracruz. She repeats the names as she buttons her white ruffled shirt, shifting her hips to the rhythm of triumph. Suki summons Octavio, her sword boy, to help her tug on her glittering, ribs-high breeches, holding her breath as he zips up the front.

Her embroidered vest comes next, night sky against her chest, enhancing her silhouette. The pink stockings spotlight her high-muscled calves. Then come her black slippers—left first, then right—and finally, her dazzling fitted jacket, fourteen pounds of coup de grâce: epaulets, brocade, loops of braided gold. Today she tucks a picture of her mother, an old passport photo, inside her *montera*. Suki kisses her fingertips, touches them to her mother's face, and prays: *Ayúdame hoy*. She smoothes her hairline with water before wedging on the *montera* in front of the armoire mirror. Suki is pleased. She looks amphibious in her suit, as if she could slay sharks as well as bulls.

All movement freezes as the lady matador emerges from the elevator in her bullfighting finery, the sword boy at her side.

There's a wedding party in the lobby, en route to the garden with its literary parrots and gargantuan malanga vines. Suki catches a glimpse of the bride trussed up in lace, false lashes grazing her brows. The bride and her entourage stare at the lady matador, fusing them for an instant. *"¡Que viva la matadora!"* the groom shouts out, but nobody echoes his sentiment. Suki suspects that this outburst will cost the groom a satisfactory honeymoon.

As she strides under the crystal webs of chandeliers to the front revolving doors, her coruscating suit seems to shoot off stars. The concierge, unflappable as ever in his starched *guayabera,* is the only one with sufficient wits to bid the lady matador "a productive afternoon." She nods, rewarding him with a half smile. Everyone else—bellhops, shop owners, military brass, the Spanish ambassador and his wife, security guards, marble polishers, down to the last smartly attired guest—is stunned into silence. Suki looks neither right nor left as she proceeds through the lobby. To speak, she knows, would break the spell of the toreador.

The limousine ride to the ring is torturously slow, prolonged by the traffic and political protesters on every corner. Suki glances at their posters but doesn't absorb their meanings. Octavio knows to stay silent. Right now Suki must remain focused on her body, in the long, lean muscles of her thighs, the girdle of strength in her waist and hips. Suki's had only two serious mishaps in the ring: a goring that left a nine-inch scar on her thigh; and a fractured sacrum, the result of being stomped on by a bull. Both incidents happened when she was an apprentice, fighting her first twenty-five battles in dusty small-town rings.

There's no room for error or distraction, Suki thinks. Who can afford it? With each goring, the matadors say, a few drops of courage seep out. In the ring, ultimately, it comes to this: pitting muscle and cunning against bigger muscles. Without the bull, the matador is nothing. There's no drama, no spectacle, no poetry. Without the bull, there is no glory. No immortality. In giving the bull a chance to fight for its life, everyone is redeemed.

The stadium is nearly three-quarters full, not bad for a mid-week fight. Suki takes in the crowd, which has more women in it than usual. Many wear outlandish hats, wave signs in her support: A WOMAN'S PLACE IS IN THE RING! MAKE TAMALES, NOT WAR! ENOUGH BULL—FIGHT! The picadors report that busloads of women dressed in their Sunday best—mothers and daughters, with *abuelitas* in tow—were dropped off at the entrance early, where they were admitted for half price.

"So much for the fairer sex's aversion to violence," Melvyn croaks, and Luís laughs.

After the opening fanfare, the picadors mount their padded, blindfolded horses and enter the ring. Suki doesn't like the looks of this bull; not now, not earlier when she and her men visited the stalls for a morning preview. She heard that *el toro* came from a breeding ranch across the border to the south, that its stock is unstable. Suki watches Melvyn and Luís work in tandem to weaken the bull with their lances. Only once does it lunge at them halfheartedly, favoring its right horn. Grunting, Luís repeatedly strikes the bull between its shoulders before his horse, a born clown, prances backward, entertaining the crowd.

The wind changes direction twice, bringing with it the smell of jasmine and fried pork rinds from the far corners of the capital. An ambulance sounds in the distance. The *banderilleros* are up next. Manolo and Paco look like twins from afar—stout and strong-buttocked in their silvery suits, with arms that never completely rest at their sides. Octavio, who joins them, is only half their size. All three are tireless with their colorful barbed poles, but the bull is indifferent to their attacks, as if they were merely a nuisance, a trio of droning mosquitoes. Their performance isn't doing what it's supposed to: creating the density of suspense necessary for her entrance. It seems to Suki that the bull is conserving its strength for a worthier opponent.

The spectators cheer when the lady matador finally steps into the center of the ring. The sequins of her *traje de luz* gleam in the sun. Suki circles in place, her *montera* held high, to acknowledge her fans. Aromas of churros and cheap beer waft toward her from the weather-beaten stands. The vendors' calls float out across the ring. "Lemonade!" "Meat rolls!" "Balloons!" Unused to the high-pitched wails of adoring women, Suki must redouble her focus. Their snapping fans clatter like a chorus of castanets.

The afternoon light glues the fitful beast to the dust. Suki stands still, taking its measure beneath the clear November sky. A net of blood oozes from its bulging neck, where the picadors lanced hard. The barbed poles bounce and click, flailing like stiff, waving arms. The bull's sides, too, are saturated with blood. It's reacting oddly, refusing to meet her gaze. Even after the lady matador flagrantly whips her cape in front of its face, the bull ignores her. A bad sign. Perhaps it's nothing but a coward, pretending aloofness—dangerous and unpredictable, the worst of its kind.

Out of the corner of her eye, Suki notices the tarnished cymbals in the orchestra. Will they incite the bull to action?

After an eternity, the bull lifts its head and looks at the lady matador almost tenderly. How much easier it would be to let it live. Of course, she cannot permit this. Suki breathes deeply, down into her pelvis. The *banderilleros* encourage her from the sidelines. "Win his confidence first," they advise. "Don't make any sudden moves." The bull, glossy with sweat and coagulating blood, snorts and fixes a stare on the box row of journalists, as if intending to send them skyward toward the dimmest of planets. Then it trots off in the opposite direction.

The heat collects at the small of Suki's back. Her underarms burn and her wrists are stiff with tension. This bull, she thinks, is making a fool of her. It turns and faces her again, its nostrils moistly black. The beast moves forward, as if it's going to attack, then just as quickly stops. The spectators begin shouting, taunting it to charge. One *borracho* insults the lady matador, goads her to do something, anything, to prove she belongs in the ring. "Let's see what you're made of, *princesa*!" But the women shout him down.

Suki approaches the bull again, her shadow jerking behind her, the red muleta rippling from the force of her stride. The beast is motionless, wary, swelling in the heat. Its eyes look as flat as two buttons. It follows the lady matador's progress, looking bemused, as if it can't believe a creature so lithe and gleaming would dare come this close.

"This is between you and me," Suki whispers. She removes her *montera* and tosses it at the bull. The velvety hat soars through the air, landing inches from the beast's muzzle. Still, it doesn't charge.

The lady matador ventures closer, sets her legs apart, left foot slightly in front of her right. Again, she offers *el toro* her cape. The beast stirs, reconsidering its indifference, then charges with all its might. Suki hooks the cape before swinging it ahead of the bull, her arms low. Its right horn passes close to her waist. *"¡Olé!"*

the crowd hollers as she passes the bull out with the cape. She flips the cape and the bull passes her on the other side. A classic *verónica*.

Suki repeats this over and again. On the fifth turn, the bull passes so close that it smears her breeches with a strip of bloody rosettes, marking the place she was once gored. Then she turns her back on the beast to show who's in control. Suki lures the bull toward her twice more, kneeling first on one leg, then the other, swooping the crimson cape low. The crowd goes wild.

A chanting starts up among the women: *Su-ki! Su-ki! Su-ki!* Soon the whole stadium thunders with shouting, clapping, stamping. The orchestra joins in, tubas and trombones, snare drums and trumpets, all beating out her name.

For an instant, the sun blinds the lady matador but she doesn't take her eyes off the bull. With utmost focus, she pulls the cape toward her, hands stained from the blood-soaked muleta, and winds the bull around her like an opulent sash. This, more than anything, will tire it. The bull fumbles, loses its balance, recovers. It's breathing hard now, its sides heaving. A terrible bellows.

When the lady matador is certain the bull is fixed in place, she motions for Octavio. The crowd grows quiet as Suki accepts the thin, curved sword. She considers the weary bull, its horns low, and carefully aims the blade. She must finish this quickly, honorably. No sooner does Suki lift the sword high and move in for the kill than the beast plunges a horn into her ribs, easily, as if into pudding. Then it tosses her over its head as if she were a rag doll. Suki lands on the bull's bloody back, dislodging two barbs, before rolling into the ring amid an odor so savage and enveloping it can only mean death.

Fire races under her skin, a painful flowering. *The grotesque always precedes the sublime.* Her *tía* Chofi, who slept with a crucifix clenched to her breast, used to tell her this.

Shouts from her *cuadrilla* ricochet around the lady matador. Her men rush in with the vast pink capes to lure away the heat and muscle of the bull. It stampedes them, furious, but they manage to evade its horns. *El toro* will die less gloriously now, its few privileges lost. Suki can't move her body but she sees her mother's face in the clouds. Her head drops to one side and she notices the scribbled trail of blood in the ring, hieroglyphs, a message she must read. Her vision is blurring, and in the pitiless logic of the moment, she fears she might die without learning its hidden code.

Four men in white, like bearded angels—maybe they *are* angels?—lift her heavenward. One of them looks like a bleached photograph of her *abuelo* Ramón; another resembles her sword boy, though aged by twenty years. Neither of them, to her knowledge, ever sported a beard. Suki longs to offer them eggs, perfect ones still warm from hens. She spies rose petals fluttering through the air, scenting her breath. *Ay,* how she blooms, blooms, blooms toward nothingness.

The Hospital

It all begins and ends with sound. No lives are saved, no hunger is alleviated, no rent is paid or children clothed. Yet poetry is as essential to his life as air. In the last twenty-four hours, Ricardo has written nine poems in the hospital—the beginnings of what he hopes will be an autobiographical epic. If he had the luxury of staying a year, he might write an entire cycle of books.

Today, the poet wants to compose a pantoum about the Mariel exodus, about his voyage from Cuba to Key West on a tugboat piloted by deranged exiles. He appreciates the pantoum's languor, the way the quatrains move forward and back, old-fashioned as a *danzón,* perfect for evoking the vacillations of the past.

Ricardo rolls a pencil between his thumb and forefinger, searching the hospital room for a place to start. He notices the exposed gums of the patient by the window, the opaque tube in his throat, mottled, like a dying tree. The patient lights a cigarette and begins smoking through the hole in his throat. Ricardo says nothing, though the smoke irritates his eyes. As a child, his mother's incessant smoking used to send him to the hospital with asthma attacks. He had to take daily walks along the *malecón* to fill his lungs with countervailing fresh air.

Another patient, in the bed next to his, scrabbles for the remote control and turns on the TV to a blaring level. A noisome game show is under way. Contestants are dressed as billiard balls and collide with one another on a huge pool table. The host, ridiculous and tuxedoed with a slick pompadour, gyrates to an old Bee Gees hit. Ricardo is on the verge of complaining when the patient switches channels to the midday news report. The latest election poll shows the ex-dictator gaining on the front-runner by promising each voter a fifty-dollar cash rebate. The American ambassador, his tie askew, vows to hunt down whoever murdered his consular officer. The lady matador is giving a preview fight at the municipal bullring this afternoon.

Ricardo understands *la matadora* better now. To face death and survive is to fill oneself to bursting with imperious life. *Todo que fui / no existe más.* He scribbles this on a prescription pad, scratches it out, rests his pen on one knee. The machine next to him beeps encouragingly, its lines spiking like an optimistic business chart. Perhaps he should write an elegy to his former life, a sestina to cheating death. Or an ode to fatherhood, at long last fulfilled.

The poet closes his eyes and massages his forehead, trying to coax forth another pretty garland of words. Lyrics from old Rolling Stones songs keep floating through his head. When he was a teenager, Ricardo translated into Spanish bootlegged copies of the *Sticky Fingers* and *Let It Bleed* albums, liberally interpreting the lyrics with a secondhand dictionary. In those days, he wore bell bottoms that he'd tie-dyed and sewn from his mother's kitchen curtains.

The nurse waddles in with the poet's lunch. Ricardo finds the swishing sound of her white panty hose soothing somehow, and half expects her legs to give off sparks. She adjusts the angle of his bed, then checks the bandage on his chest. Her name is Marta. She is wider than she is tall, with a kindly face and a brusque, professional manner. Her upper lip is furred like a bee. She insists that Ricardo try the unappetizing pork tamales, to build up his strength.

"You're not one of those vegetarians, are you?" Marta asks with suspicion when he shows no interest in his food.

Ricardo wants to retort that a meal of pork tamales and refried beans isn't optimal for someone recovering from a knife wound, but he doesn't want to upset her. "Would you happen to have more paper?"

"Planning to write to the president, eh? Go complaining about crime in the capital?" Marta tucks in a corner of the bed and refills the water pitcher. "That's the first thing tourists do when a mosquito bites them."

"It was hardly a mosquito bite, Señora!"

"Now don't get indignant on me. You got off easy, I hope you know that. If one of those *mara* gangs had gotten hold of you, there'd be a million little pieces of you for the mongrels to devour."

Ricardo clears his throat. "Any paper?"

"You know, I had to memorize poems in grade school. Do you know the one that begins . . . Ah, let's see . . . *The swan composed of snow—*"

"*—floats in shadow, amber beak translucent in the last light.*"

"Yes, that's it!" Her round face shines. She closes the door and unsheathes a small hammer from her nurse's smock. "I could fracture your kneecaps, if you want. It'd keep you here longer."

"No, but thanks just the same."

Ricardo remembers a dream from his morning nap. In it, he was peeling shrimp on Varadero Beach, trying to sell a bucket's worth to sunburned German tourists. His fingers bled and stank of the sea.

He picks up his pen again. It's crucial that he convey the desperation he felt leaving Cuba. His wife was pregnant. Most of his friends were in jail. His mother had just had her left leg amputated below the knee. Ricardo brought two books with him on that one-way trip to Florida: a collection of Rubén Darío and another of José Martí. On the crossing over, a fight broke out and a stump of a man with a tattoo of La Virgen de la Caridad del Cobre on his forearm threw another man overboard.

The doctor stops by for one last exam before signing the poet's release form. Ricardo detests this decorous fellow. Dr. Conejo attended medical school in Havana in the 1970s, during the

worst of the persecutions. Ricardo was imprisoned then, enduring "reeducation" mixed with beatings, and force-fed psycho-
tropic drugs. Half the time, he was high on the revolution's dime.

The propaganda included such absurdities as venerating
Margarita, the cow with phenomenal udders that broke milk-
production records on the Isle of Pines. Margarita was even
brought, mooing vulgarly, to Ricardo's prison to inspire the
inmates. "El Comandante says we all need to follow this heifer's
example," the warden pronounced.

"What do you hear of your friend?" Ricardo sneers.

"Which friend is that?" The doctor doesn't look up from his
chart, scribbling something in red ink.

"*Tu amigo, El Comandante.*" Ricardo sits upright in his hospital bed.

"I'm neither his friend nor his attending physician, so I
wouldn't know." The doctor's demeanor is unassailable. He looks
at the poet without a hint of rancor and wishes him a pleasant
stay in the country.

The poet moves to the edge of the bed, frustrated by the
encounter. For him, there's nothing like a good quarrel to seduce
the muse. He takes a last stab at writing his pantoum: *As the
island fades / I leave behind departure itself.* He scratches this
out in disgust. Ricardo gathers his things and shuffles down
the hospital corridor, one shoe untied. Sarah promised to meet
him back at the hotel. She's angry with him for getting stabbed
in the first place. His wife suspects that everything he does is a
scheme to avoid responsibility. Little Isabel, at least, will be glad
to see him. He can't wait to feel the sweet weight of her head
against his chest.

Several wrong turns later, the poet walks into the emergency department of the hospital. The doors swing open and the lady matador is brought in on a stretcher. She's conscious but the sheet covering her is soaked in blood. She looks gorgeous, a wounded saint. He would canonize her himself, if he could. Ricardo waves, trying to catch her attention, but she doesn't notice him. An orderly ushers him outdoors, into the smog and grime of the capital. The late afternoon clouds are darkening, as if on schedule, and a sheet of lightning illuminates the sky.

The News

From Radio Novedades

Has ecological terrorism reached new extremes? That's the concern of loggers in the remote jungle areas of Carmelita, which has undergone rapid deforestation in recent years. According to eyewitness reports, blue-bellied monkeys the size of humans—believed by some to be leftist activists in disguise—have killed two workmen, raided campsites, and dragged off construction supplies in the dead of night. Simian specialists from around the globe are rushing to this remote logging site on the chance that these blue-bellied beasts might, in fact, be a prehistoric species of monkey flushed out of their jungle habitat. "Old Mayan texts refer to carnivorous nocturnal monkeys of a strange blue hue," says Dr. Francisco Morelia, chair of the anthropology department at the College of San Miguel. "But it remains unclear whether they were mythic or actual creatures."

From *El Nuevo Tiempo*

Painter and performance artist Alba "Frida" Montenegro was arrested in front of the Justice Department yesterday for disrupting the peace. Carrying a bucket of pigs' blood into which she periodically dipped her feet, Ms. Montenegro left a trail of bloody footprints around the building before police forcibly removed her from the premises. By then a crowd had gathered, demanding: "Let her walk! Let her walk!"

According to Ms. Montenegro, the footprints represent "an artistic response to the swinish crimes committed and upheld by our so-called judicial system during our country's long civil war." As she was led away, the unruly artist cried out: "Only beauty will save us from the abyss!"

From Channel 9's *Top of the News*

Thousands of mourners are expected this weekend at the memorial service of Federico Ladrón-Benes, president of the Universal Fruit Company, who died in a plane crash in the Caribbean earlier this week. Preliminary examination of recovered plane fragments suggests the possibility of high-powered explosives. No one has stepped forward to claim responsibility for the blast, though officials say they're certain leftist terrorists are to blame . . .

From Radio INFO1210

The voices of our gay population were heard loud and clear today during a parade in the lakeside tourist town of Punto

Lago. A few of the protesters marched in drag, while others sported the lavender overalls that have become the hallmarks of *el movimiento* gay. Tourists encouraged the protesters, who are demanding equality before the law and an end to AIDS. Local vendors reported a surge in sales of rainbow T-shirts. Pedro Zayas, who owns a souvenir shop that sells jaguar masks and Mayan calendar key chains, said: "It's up to God to judge these *patos*. But for us here in Punto Lago, they're definitely good for business."

From *The Lupe Galeano Show*

Lupe Galeano: Oh, my, my, my, you're in for a special treat! We have with us today none other than the resplendent Paloma Gómez. She's come to our fair capital to compete in the first ever Battle of the Lady Matadors. Ladies and gentlemen, please help me welcome Mexico's greatest living bullfighter!

[*Audience applause*]

I'm sooo delighted that you could make it, Paloma. I know how busy you must be preparing for Sunday's fight.

Paloma Gómez: I've been training pretty hard for this—

L.G.: You look marvelous, darling! So svelte! Doesn't she, audience?

[*Fervent applause*]

Do tell us your secrets for staying in such enviable shape . . .

P.G.: Well, it's not exactly the sort of thing the average person does.

L.G.: *Pero claro,* Paloma, that's why we want to know!

P.G.: Okay then. I warm up with a ten-mile run every morning. Then I work out with weights for ninety minutes. Most days, I follow that with a mile swim in the ocean—

L.G.: Why, I'm huffing and puffing just listening to you!

P.G.: I also train with a boxing coach, who helps me with my footwork and general dexterity. And then I get in the ring with a bull.

L.G. (*leaning toward her guest*): Can I feel your arm muscles? Oooooh! You won't be easy to beat. I presume you've heard about Suki?

P.G.: I saw the replays. But knowing her, she'll be back in time for the fight.

LG: You two are bitter rivals, I understand.

P.G.: Let's just say Suki keeps things interesting for all of us in the ring.

L.G. (*sotto voce*): And outside, too, no? Her, eh, *exploits* are legendary, are they not . . . ?

CHAPTER FIVE

El coreano *goes to a funeral • The lady matador receives guests at the hospital • The ex-guerrilla's quandary • The lawyer takes drastic action • The news*

THURSDAY

Listen to me as one listens to the rain . . .

—Octavio Paz

Funeral Home

Won Kim looks up at the void of windless sky before entering
the marble foyer of the mortuary. There is no trace of the hurricane that was predicted. A rose-throated tanager whirs overhead
and settles in the jacaranda tree across the street. A beggar stands
under it, rigid as a totem pole, a tattered bowler on his head.
Only his jaws move as he gnaws on a strip of jerked beef. Beyond
the jacaranda, a tower of cumulus clouds drifts slowly west.

At the funeral home, a somber man offers to take Won Kim's
hat. Another ushers him into the viewing room, where the corpses

of the six Korean businessmen were hastily put on display. They look garish to him, immodest in their expensive silk suits, laid out for all the world to see. Tomorrow they will be transported back to their families in Korea. There is no justice for what happens in the world, Won Kim thinks. It seems to him that those desperate to stay alive are infinitely more adept at dying than he.

Won Kim greets the other mourners with a weak smile. Mr. Choi's face is partly bandaged with gauze. A manufacturer of shoddy handbags, Mr. Choi was with the deceased the night of the fire but survived because he was taking a piss in the parking lot. Mr. Chong and Mr. Park are also here, wearing hemp cloth armbands.

"We're s-s-sorry to hear of your troubles," Mr. Park says with a solicitous stammer. "Your f-f-ather would've—"

"Troubles can be resolved, death cannot," Won Kim cuts him off. He refuses to discuss his so-called troubles with either of them.

"Have you heard about the lady matador?" Mr. Chong asks, changing the subject. "She was gored by a bull and still vows to fight!"

"What a woman," Mr. Park chimes in, worried over having offended Won Kim. "It's a wonder she d-d-didn't die in the ring."

"A pity to waste so much beauty on a bull," Mr. Chong chortles, all rictus. "She could be *personally* helping us with the global economy—ha!"

Won Kim is disgusted with the turn of the conversation. Mr. Chong and Mr. Park were friends of his father's years ago, when he had cut a memorable figure throughout the Americas. Won Kim forces himself to imagine the three of them stranded in an ill-made boat far out to sea, the gods of thunder hard-drumming their demise. This calms Won Kim and he shifts his attention to the dead men before him.

Death is the ultimate solution to everything, he thinks, the most elegant. People linger much too long and uselessly in life, bellowing over insignificances. The loveliest things in the world are the most fleeting. Blossoming cherry trees. The twilight hour. Rare butterflies that live no more than a day or two. For a heart-stopping moment these creatures saturate time, then they, too, expire.

Last night, to Won Kim's consternation, his mistress embroidered a glorious monarch butterfly on the sleeve of his hotel bathrobe. Berta told him that in the Highlands, people understood that the world of dreams and the world of work are twin realities, like the opposing wings of a butterfly. The wings must connect at the butterfly's heart for it to live and fly, she said, biting off a length of thread.

Won Kim stands by the caskets of the dead men (five of the six are open; the last is closed due to disfiguring burns). He knew one of the businessmen quite well. Yi Chul started out with Won Kim at his father's company fifteen years ago. During their first months on the job they spent their free time together, going drinking after work and double-dating pretty sisters. When Won Kim was sent to the tropics, Yi Chul was transferred to Tokyo, a coveted post. Later, he was fired for embezzling two hundred thousand dollars. How Yi Chul managed to flourish in spite of this debacle remains a mystery.

Won Kim leans over his ex-friend's corpse and examines the thick length of his body, cushioned in ivory satin. His fat fingers are enlaced at his waist, a wedding band wedged in place. His face looks as smugly confident as it did in life. He, too, kept a mistress in the tropics while his wife and children remained in Seoul. The last thing Yi Chul could have imagined was that he would perish in a seedy nightclub ten thousand miles from home.

After the fire, the nightclub was immediately sold to a developer for next to nothing. Won Kim heard that Yi Chul's company had arranged the sale to avoid a scandal. In six months, with a bit of lumber and a splash of paint, nobody would remember the Happy Feet nightclub, or the Korean businessmen who died there watching naked girls slide up and down a greased pole.

The walls of the chapel are dispiritingly white. The chaplain drones on in his Sunday Spanish. Won Kim wonders how many of those in attendance are familiar with the traditional ways. In Korea, the mourning period used to last three years. On the day his own grandfather died, Won Kim's eldest uncle climbed on the roof of their house and called out the old man's name. Won Kim was five years old at the time. He was nine before the cloud of mourning finally lifted from his family's home. In the interim, everyone had forgotten how to laugh.

After his own father died, the family put three spoonfuls of rice in his mouth and laid new coins on his tongue. They wrapped his body in *suii,* the traditional death dress, and erected a shrine in his honor. And every year on the anniversary of his death, they hold a memorial service for him. This is how a good family honors its dead. As a boy, Won Kim had fantasized about preserving his father in a formaldehyde solution, as he'd done with his finest specimens. No bruises, or punctures, or torn wings. It was the only way he could think of to save his butterfly collection. Remembering this makes him more despondent still.

Won Kim settles in the back pew of the chapel and removes a pen from his breast pocket. It feels like a brick of gold in his hand. Perhaps the gods of suicide will favor him today. He composes a note on the back of the funeral program. *Dearest sisters, I am neither useful nor pleasing and I boast no special talents. Is it a crime then to hasten the inevitable?* Won Kim wants to add that he has already lost everything, that his life has been wasted. But this would hurt his sisters too much. *Please do not blame yourselves. I do this of my own volition. In the end, love has eluded me.*

Won Kim scratches out this last line. If he is not going to be honest in his suicide note, then there is no point in writing one. The truth is that he fell in love twice: First when he was fifteen, with a girl two years his senior, long-legged and startlingly muscled, who ignored him completely. The second time was in Thailand, with a sales clerk in an electronics shop. Every day for a month, Won Kim visited her, buying pointless gadgets—transformers, and regulators to fix equipment he did not own—so his hands could caress what her fingers had briefly touched. When she quit without warning, nobody in the shop would tell him where she had gone.

Won Kim's hands go limp with the memory. If only he had worked up the courage to properly court that Thai girl, he would not be sitting here pretending to mourn the dead. At times he can barely contain the wildness of regret inside him. He is convinced that nothing that happens in public is of any truthful value. Whatever drama and meaning life holds takes place behind closed doors, or deep inside the bloody chambers of the heart.

Won Kim stands up, coughs discreetly, and steps out of the chapel into the grim corridors of the funeral home. As he reaches the front door, the same man who took his hat returns it to him. Won Kim crosses the street, fedora in hand, and narrowly dodges a dairy truck. It distresses him how his instincts defy his intentions, working continuously to keep him alive.

As he reaches the park, the beggar, who has been standing under the jacaranda tree all along, unexpectedly drops a stone into his hat. Won Kim stares at the man, who grins back at him with blackened gums. Won Kim peers into his hat. The stone is perfectly oval, egglike, a brilliant blue.

"Gracias," he says, digging in his pocket for a coin. Instead he takes out a wad of bills and gives it to the man, who, Won Kim suddenly realizes, is missing a leg, or half of it anyway, just above the knee. "I won't be needing this," he mumbles to the one-legged man, and turns toward the hotel.

Hospital

The lady matador opens her eyes after an uncomfortable nap. The coarse hospital sheets make her legs itch. The dingy room magnifies everything: the thrum of the monitoring equipment, the nurses arguing down the hall, the crumbs on her plastic breakfast tray. Suki is convinced that she can hear her ribs aching, too, though they feel oddly remote to her, like they belong to someone else. She has an unbearable urge to rip off her bandages and finger the wound in her ribs, feel its torn edges, the mark of the bull.

Suki consoles herself by humming a song she loved as a child, a folk tune her Japanese grandmother used to sing to her. *Mori no fukoro ga iimashita watashi wa mori no mihari yaku . . . The forest owl said, "I am the guardian of the forest, fearsome wolves and the like won't be allowed to come near" . . .* So why is it, Suki wonders, that she's made a career of seeking out fear itself? Her mother took her to Yokohama twice, each time for a month. Suki remembers eating hot soup with tofu for breakfast when all she wanted was Cap'n Crunch. By the end of each visit, Suki was fluent in Japanese but her fluency evaporated soon after she returned to the States.

Today the lady matador feels better than yesterday. At least she can breathe without growing nauseous. Already she is restless for action. Every minute feels to her like a tiny blue flame in danger of being snuffed out.

After the goring, Suki was surrounded by journalists who complained when she didn't give them a quote. Well, they came for high drama and she gave it to them—even more than they could've hoped for. She lost a bucket of blood but miraculously no organs were damaged. Her grandfather had been gored so severely in Zaragoza that he spent the rest of his life in a wheelchair, the throne from which he relived and retold his stories. Her story might've ended similarly.

Suki thinks of her *cuadrilla* back at the hotel, waiting for their big break to come with hers. They've taken an enormous risk linking their fortunes to a woman. She doesn't know what they'll do if she decides to quit.

In the far corner of the room, Suki spots a set of immense, pimply buttocks framed by a hospital gown. The buttocks belong to a patient standing by the window and waving her arms to someone outside. The patient flashes her hands five times. Suki suspects that she's making a deal with reporters in the parking lot.

"What the hell are you doing?" she demands.

The patient shrieks and accidentally knocks a hand through the window, shattering glass. A pair of nurses barge in with clipboards. They notice the broken window and the patient's bloodied hand and call for security. In no time the room is swarming with orderlies and guards pointing their guns every which way, trying to figure out whom to shoot. The half-naked patient is whisked away, wailing, on a gurney. Suki catches the eye of an orderly, a well-built *moreno* just her type. She could do worse than getting a precompetition workout with him.

Suki smells her father for a whole minute before she sees him. Papi's been using the same aftershave for as long as she can remember. It's called Glacier and comes in a bottle shaped like an ice floe, tinted a piercing blue. It's meant to conjure up Nordic lands but for Suki the scent is pure tropics: mangoes and rice pudding, dancing mambos in Veracruz's humid heat.

After her parents divorced, Suki saw her father only at Christmas and for summer vacations. But the Palacios clan ferociously claimed her. Tía Chofi, in particular, took Suki under her wing. Together they made sugar candy and dried it on sheets of glass on the roof. Tía Chofi was handy with a needle, too, and sewed fashionable wardrobes for Suki's action figures. She was the only kid whose GI Joes wore embroidered evening gowns.

"*¡Mi amor!*" Papi roars as he enters her room. His pants are snug and his hair is dyed black as a beetle's. "I was beside myself when I heard the news! We were crossing the border in that stinking tin can of a bus when someone turned up the radio. 'That's my daughter!' I shouted but nobody believed me. You know, *hija*, you're quite celebrated in these parts."

Suki half grins, half grimaces. Her father is holding her too tight but it's been months since they've seen each other and she doesn't want him to stop. Suki looks past his shoulder at his new girlfriend. Her face looks pulled to one side, like a flounder's. It's either an optical illusion, or a plastic surgery mishap. The woman wears a loud flowered dress with a matching purse and shoes. If an exact opposite of her mother could exist, Suki thinks, this woman would be it.

"This is Rosa." Papi turns and coaxes her forward. "My fiancée."

Rosa slips off a meshed glove and offers up a manicured claw, taking note of Suki's chewed cuticles. Suki looks at her father, who averts his gaze. She checks her temper by mentally quizzing herself on the arteries of the upper extremity: right subclavian artery, vertebral artery, suprascapular artery . . .

"I brought you something," Rosa chirps, unwrapping a crumpled package and brandishing it like a trophy. It's a statue of Saint Lazarus, complete with miniature crutch and leprous feet. "Isn't he gorgeous?"

"Rosa is devoted to him," Papi says morosely. "Tell her about the miracle *que*—"

"Actually, I'm feeling kind of tired." Suki tries to feign a yawn but it hurts her ribs too much. "I need to get my rest for Sunday." She wants this visiting hour to be over immediately.

Part of a dream from last night resurfaces, blocking out flounder woman's chatter. In the dream, Suki and her mother are in their apartment in Santa Monica. It's winter and everything looks crisply clean. Her mother's bed is an operating table, a kind of surgical theater, and Suki is the doctor. She makes an incision in her mother's left shoulder and, with a huge syringe, pumps glue into her skeletal system, trying to paste her frail bones together. Her mother is silent, martyrlike. What Suki is doing is excruciating but her mother doesn't complain.

"You're still going to fight?" Rosa's oversized mouth forms a perfect O. Suki wishes she could stopper it with something—the float ball from a toilet tank would do. "My father used to say that if you can kill the memory, you can kill the pain."

"That would be a lot of forgetting in your case, wouldn't—"

"Can you return to the ring so soon?" Papi jumps in. Suki can tell he's uneasy but pleased by her determination to fight. "I would hate to see you end up like Abuelo Ramón. *Ay,* that man never stopped dreaming of the ring!"

A rattle of drums rises up from the street. Papi goes to the broken window and peers outside. "It's a wedding procession," he says, "or a funeral."

"Same difference," Suki mutters. After Sunday's bullfight, she'll enlist her great-aunt to break these two lovebirds apart. Even bedridden, it'll take Tía Chofi about thirty seconds to send this vulture packing.

"Rogelio and I are planning a fairy-tale wedding." Rosa sighs, inspecting her manicure. "Four hundred people, a choir of angels, a carriage pulled by white stallions, and my absolutely favorite—"

"Tía Chofi sends her love, *hija.*" Papi interrupts his fiancée this time. "She wants to see you before her kidneys give out."

With her great-aunt's blessing, Suki fought her first calf when she was fourteen. "In the bullring, you dominate death, bring it to its knees," Tía Chofi said. "In the ring and the ring alone, you impose your terms."

"Maybe I'll go back with you to Veracruz after the tournament."

"You mean after you *win* the tournament, no?" Papi laughs. His girlfriend joins in, echoing the pitch of his voice.

"Of course," Suki agrees. "After I win."

A knock on the door startles them both. It's Paloma Gómez, looking magisterial in an aquamarine pantsuit with myriad buckles.

Papi sputters like a rusty motor but emits nothing coherent.

"I've come to offer my condolences," Paloma says, her hatchet nose high in the air. She surveys the hospital room as if trying to determine the best line of attack.

"I'm not dead yet," Suki counters. She'd rather be stark naked in front of Paloma than in this shit-green hospital gown. It's intolerable to her that she appear even the slightest bit vulnerable.

"Yes, I can see you're very much alive."

"Even half dead, she'll wipe the arena with you!" Papi finally blurts out.

"Dad, please."

"Don't think we don't know what tricks you've perpetrated on—"

"Now I know where you get your, eh, spirit." Paloma bares her gums like a horse.

"—the unsuspecting public! *Desgraciada*. You'll end up behind bars, if I have anything to do with it."

Paloma ignores his outburst and turns to Rosa, who looks like a wilted peony in the corner. "Ah, and this is your backup? Even the blindest of bulls will have no trouble finding her in the ring."

"Your time here is up," Suki pronounces, fixing a deadly gaze on La Paloma. "We'll decide this in the ring." Then she dismisses her nemesis with a wave of the hand.

"In the ring, *querida*," Paloma echoes as she strides out of the room.

Roof

The capital looks different every time Aura surveys it from the hotel rooftop—buildings destroyed or constructed, trees toppled, old roads repaved, a hodgepodge of church spires and dilapidated huts. For the most part, the city is a cemetery of worn-out things, divided by smoke and trash. To the west are the mansions, big enough to trace with a fingertip. To the north loom the blue-black volcanoes: impassive, threatening ruin.

Below her, vendors shout out what's for sale: transistor radios, cones of candy-roasted peanuts, sandals made in China they swear will last till Judgment Day. A milk truck, honking loudly, careens around a man shuffling toward the park, hat in hand. Aura recalls her first days in the city. Her eyes wanted to take in everything but her ears suffered from the constant noise. It was rarely silent in the jungle but at least each sound was distinct—howler monkey, gunshot, machete thwack. Here noise melds together into earsplitting dissonance. It's unusual to make out a single birdsong.

The wind blows hard, stirring the leaves in the street, stripping the last petals off the bougainvillea. Aura slept restlessly last night and she is tired to her bones. She yawns, examining her tray. The hot chocolate she brought for Julio is growing cold. She licks off the melting whipped cream and waits. Wait, waiting, waiting on. It's the verb that most defines her life. Aura is fed up with being its hostage. If only she could fold back time to the before, and the before, and the before the captain came to her village. Her life would be completely different now. She wouldn't be living in the capital. She wouldn't be working as a waitress. And she certainly wouldn't be loitering on a hotel rooftop waiting for instructions from her dead brother.

It occurs to Aura grimly that men are still determining her days, only now she's serving both the living and the dead. *You'll know yourself by remembering your dreams.* Julio told her this once but she isn't sure what it means. Only her nightmares resemble her waking life. Aura smoothes her pink-and-white apron, with its ample double pockets. She detects the fragrance of sweet buns from the Tres Leches bakery. Her lover, Juan Carlos, used to dream of sweet buns in the jungle and salivate in his sleep. *Ay,* she must stop inhabiting the past. The big question, the one she needs to decide today, is this: Should she kill one man, or fifty?

The door to the roof bangs open and a disturbed-looking *chinito* stands blinking in the unforgiving sun. He looks familiar to her but she can't quite place him, or remember his name. He holds his hat in one hand and a blue rock in the other, staring as blankly as a sleepwalker. Suddenly, he grins at her sweetly, innocently, with the face of eternal childhood. Aura keeps still, afraid to rupture his trance.

"How long will you be here?" he asks, slipping the stone into his jacket pocket.

Without waiting for a response, he sprints toward the edge of the roof and takes to the air like a seagull. He hovers there, strangely graceful, as if held by unseen strings, his arms and legs splayed in surrender. For a moment, Aura does nothing, believing it's an apparition. Stranger things have happened on this roof. But a streak of dread runs through her and she knows she must act. Aura lunges after the *chinito,* managing to grab hold of his ankles. She pulls him down hard and he smacks against the side of the building. Aura hangs on as he dangles there, heavy as a sack of yams. Her knees dig into the roof tar, her elbows and chin get badly scraped. Her life, she fears, depends on saving his.

Just when Aura can't hang on a second longer, a hot draft of air loosens her grip. The *chinito* miraculously rights himself and, without another word, scurries through the rooftop door. Aura stands up, picking the sticky tar off her legs.

"Was this some kind of test?" she asks her brother testily.

He is rippling and indistinct as a distant stream.

"He won't have any memory of this, I can assure you."

"*Bueno,* one less thing to worry about." Aura squints in the light. "You know about the bartender's plan?"

"It's an opportunity to—"

"*Mira,* Julio. You're already dead so maybe it's not such a big deal for you." Aura spits a bit of gravel from her mouth.

"You don't have to do it, *hermana.*" Her brother's voice softens, disappointed.

"If I only knew it would stop. But it never stops." Aura recalls her father's sun-darkened arms. After a long day in the fields, he would lift her skyward until she could touch the leaves of the ceiba tree.

"Thousands are still fighting. They're sleeping in caves, in hollows, biding their time in offices and kitchens, waiting. Remember, only the grave diggers were busy before."

"Before, everyone was buried, dead or alive."

"You know," Julio's voice shifts mischievously, "I've been sending gifts to the colonel. He wants to believe they're from that lady matador, that she's secretly courting him."

"*Pero claro,*" Aura says with a sniff. "Men always think the world revolves around them."

"There are exceptions." Julio laughs.

"Is there anything between them?" Aura feels a pang of jealousy but she doesn't know toward whom.

"The colonel charged her like a bull at the pool. I don't think she was the least bit impressed."

"She's very beautiful," Aura sighs in English.

"So you're learning the enemy's language," Julio chides her, his voice fading.

Aura shrugs. "It's part of my job."

"Every heart needs its shadow."

"What's that supposed to mean?" She's growing tired of her brother's vague pronouncements.

But Julio says nothing more, gradually vanishing in a nimbus of dust. Aura walks to the roof's edge and looks down the length of Avenida Colón. She's unspeakably weary. There's that *chinito* again, crossing the street, gray fedora in hand. A truck, horn blaring, nearly runs him down as he moves toward the park, toward a one-legged beggar in a bowler hat, holding a blue stone.

In the Capital

The ceiling fan oscillates above them, stirring the few strands of hair on the attorney general's head. He's enjoying Gertrudis's predicament a little too much for her taste. Rodolfo Cañales studies the documents Hans Stüber left him before departing for Florida. The attorney general has an annoying habit of tilting his head when bemused by the misfortune of others, then strumming his fingers in the air with unseemly zeal.

Gertrudis's contacts in Miami have reported that Hans and his mistress have checked into the Fontainebleau Hotel and that

Danila ordered fried eggs and potatoes for breakfast. Her friends in immigration are working to deport the couple. With any luck, her husband and Danila will be back in the country next week. Let the perfidious Hans charm his mistress for now. In time, those two will perish like turtledoves.

"It's a tricky issue," Cañales says. "Congress is trying to put a stop—"

"You know very well why they're pushing for that law," Gertrudis snipes. "What they don't realize is that foreigners won't wait forever for these children. Do you think they'll come to adopt twelve- and thirteen-year-olds?"

"That's not the point—"

"I agree. That is another conversation entirely."

The attorney general continues shuffling through the incriminating papers, a thick stack that could wreck a hundred careers. Gertrudis permits herself a fantasy while studying Cañales: that he is lame, with angel wings, sweeping the dirt from her kitchen. This pleases her, and she waits confidently for him to finish.

"You're in a deep hole this time, Doctora."

"The world is made up of deep holes, Rudy. We'll climb out of this one just as we have all the others."

"We?"

"Damaging my reputation will only compromise yours." Gertrudis straightens the pleats of her saffron woolen skirt. "You, of all people, understand this."

Years ago she'd worked with his father, a Supreme Court judge and a pragmatist, if there ever was one. In this country, pragmatism and self-interest inevitably triumph. Surely Judge Cañales passed along these rules to his son.

"The evidence is irrefutable, I'm afraid—" Cañales tries again but he's stopped by the lawyer's upraised hand.

"There's no room for negotiation." Gertrudis taps a crocodile shoe. "Your job depends on it." Cañales knows full well that a call by her to the president would end his career that very day. What would he do then? Move to Mexico City and write a novel?

Cañales's face hardens. It's badly pitted from adolescent acne. Gertrudis remembers him as a boy at his family's ranch, carrying a goat in his arms, its feet dangling, its muzzle pressed against his neck. That same year, she grew nine inches in as many months, surpassing her father, who pronounced her *mein Baum*. For a while, nothing fit her properly so she took to wearing men's guayaberas over her slacks. In high school, they called her El Señor Presidente behind her back.

"Very well, then." Cañales rearranges his expression and hands over the folder. Then he worries a length of knotted Buddhist rope—a gift from his wife—to reduce his rising stress.

"Now that's a good boy." Gertrudis tilts her head to match his. "Things are only as hard as you make them."

On her way across town, the lawyer flips from one radio station to the next. Everyone, it seems, is obsessed by the lady matador's dramatic goring in the ring. There was a time when Gertrudis, too, captured the attention of men. The woman she once was wore emeralds inherited from her mother and had an affair with the most dashing revolutionary in the Americas. Nicolás Szorsky was better-looking and more radical than Che but, sadly, more corruptible. After the drudgery of organizing peasants, his utopian illusions gave way to the easements of bourgeois life. The last Gertrudis heard, Nicolás was living in a villa on the east side of Antibes. It's ancient history now but she can still feel the pleasure of his touch on her skin.

The lawyer turns off the radio and pats the stack of evidence beside her. In the future, she'll transfer critical records to the Cayman Islands, where she maintains her most sensitive accounts. No more paper trails. She can't afford another indiscretion on this scale. There's nothing Gertrudis hates more than indebtedness. If it were up to her, debt would flow just one way: in her direction.

She searches for the apartment building address her secretary gave her. The neighborhood looks unpromising. Pawnshops, mostly, and greasy taco pits. A pig snuffles along the curb and a vendor approaches her with a half dozen rabbits strung up on a pole. "Rabbits for hides or meat!" he shouts, practically in her ear. Two boys linger outside the pockmarked tenement in the lethargy of noon. They wear rags for pants and no shoes. A girl with a stained dress sorts pebbles in the entryway. Everything is discolored with cement dust.

"Where can I find the Flores residence?" Gertrudis asks.

One of the boys shrugs toward the courtyard. A stairwell in the back leads to a basement apartment. Gertrudis steps through the unkempt patio and down the stairs, careful not to touch the grimy walls. A cigarette smolders at the bottom.

Her secretary is waiting with her sister-in-law. Elva looks positively voluptuous next to this scrawny girl—no hips whatsoever, her belly still soft from childbirth. There's a half-eaten meringue cake on a table decorated with a plastic stork. Flies take off and land on the icing. A high narrow window looks out on the sidewalk above. The infant, only a fortnight old, sleeps on a straw mat.

"*Le presento mi cuñada,*" Elva says, nudging her sister-in-law forward. "Her name is Marisol."

"Pleased to meet you." Gertrudis smiles at the girl. "I would like to offer you my congratulations on the birth of your son."

Marisol smiles back shyly. According to Elva, her sister-in-law suffered two stillbirths before bearing this healthy boy.

"Have you discussed the arrangements?" Gertrudis asks Elva. She doesn't like taking infants into her custody whose health she hasn't verified with her own pediatricians. But she's facing a supply bottleneck she hadn't anticipated.

Elva glances at her sister-in-law, who looks at the ground. The girl picks a loose thread from the seam of her skirt. She's quiet as a weed.

"I've told her the terms: five hundred dollars to borrow her baby for one week, after which time her son will be promptly returned to her," Elva recites.

"Yes, that's correct." Gertrudis notices a pair of handsome calfskin boots interrupting the parade of shoddy footwear overhead. (She's become a creature of special tastes.) A mottled bird she hasn't noticed before starts a rat-tat-tat like machine-gun fire in a cage in the corner.

Marisol whispers something to Elva in a dialect from the Highlands.

"My sister-in-law wants to be certain that there's no confusion over whether she's selling her baby," Elva says. "This arrangement is for one week only. She says she'll keep her breasts filled with milk for little Diego."

Marisol lifts her head and Gertrudis notices the woman's eyes watering.

"Of course, my dear," the lawyer says, trying to sound reassuring.

"I'll return Diego to you personally. I can assure you that he'll have the best of care."

The couple from Tennessee arrives tomorrow and Gertrudis needs to provide them with a temporary newborn for their first visit. By the time the bureaucratic hoop-jumping is done and their paperwork churns through the courts, the lawyer will have procured a permanent child for them. Nobody will be the wiser.

The mother says something else to Elva, this time more urgently.

"She wants to know why there's no contract to sign. What proof does she have that you'll keep your promise?"

Gertrudis pauses. She needs to choose her words carefully, keep the impatience out of her voice. "Please tell your sister-in-law that nobody has questioned my integrity before. I wouldn't be in business as long as I have without it. As you know, these transactions are quite sensitive. It's best to arrange them informally. Is that clear?"

Elva translates for her sister-in-law, then stares at Gertrudis with a firm expression. "I gave her my word, Doctora."

Her secretary is a fine employee; invaluable, in fact. Gertrudis has big plans for Elva if she continues to prove herself: a raise, year-end bonuses, additional training to take over the daily workings of the business while Gertrudis spends more time in Italy. If Elva sticks with her through this trial, she might even bankroll the girl for law school.

Marisol picks up her sleeping son. He's tiny, no more than four or five pounds, and his features are swollen, mud-colored. Gertrudis knows she can make the boy look more appealing—less *poor*—with a fresh outfit and a flying-elephants blanket.

Diego squirms in his mother's arms as she loosens her blouse to nurse him. He coughs up a stringy gobbet but soon settles down to have his fill.

"Listen to him," Marisol says in hesitant Spanish. "There's a new little soul in the world."

The News

From Channel 9's *Top of the News*

An explosion rocked the lobby of the four-star Imperial Hotel today, injuring three Canadian tourists and a bellhop. Nobody has claimed responsibility for this blast or the one at the Hotel Encanto earlier this week. Here to comment is army spokesman Colonel Martín Abel: "Leftist terrorists are trying to sow confusion and fear before the elections, but, mark my words, they won't succeed. I've made it my personal mission to stop them."

From *The Voice of Korea Abroad* TV show

Reporter: We're here with our countryman, Won Kim, outside his Glorious Textiles factory just north of the capital. Protesters have accused Mr. Kim of unethical behavior and government officials here have threatened to have him deported. These charges come on the heels of the ignominious deaths of six Korean nationals at a gentlemen's club. Would you say, Mr. Kim, that Koreans are no longer welcome in paradise?

Won Kim: I am not sure that this was ever paradise, Miss Song. In any case, I do not think these events are related, only sadly coincidental. The fact is, there has been a terrible misunderstanding. I do not abuse my workers. I pay them well and treat them like family.

Reporter: Do you believe that this attack is racially motivated?

W.K.: I am convinced that it is a political ploy to deflect attention from the real problems of the country during a heavily contested election.

Reporter: Do you miss the motherland, Mr. Kim?

W.K.: Yes, I do. Very much. And I would not do anything to damage the good reputation of Koreans everywhere.

Reporter: Thank you, Mr. Kim. Up next: our report on Koreans in Central America's growing Christian movement . . .

From *El Pajarito*

Don't let a smudge of red ruin your day, ladies. If you suspect your husband of philandering with the secretary, rouge your nipples and look the other way. He'll return to you by the new moon. YOU must be the cat dangling the mouse in its jaws. More prognostications at seven. Until then, *queridos* . . .

From Radio El Pueblo

The controversy over international adoptions heats up today as Congress considers a bill that would severely curtail the export of our country's children. For the past seventy-two hours, protesters have besieged the capital with harrowing tales of baby kidnappings and the exploitation of poor, child-bearing women. Adoption lawyers are fighting back. "There's no selling of babies going on here," insists attorney Gertrudis Stüber. "The few children we manage to find good homes for abroad would otherwise be living in the streets. We're performing a great humanitarian service to these unfortunate lives."

From Radio Evangélica

The former president is in critical condition at Todos Santos Hospital today after being shot by an unknown assailant. The attack occurred shortly after our leader spoke at a rally outside a Korean textiles factory cited for the mistreatment of its workers. Your prayers, Christian soldiers, are crucial for getting the general back on his feet in time to win the election. The general issued this statement to supporters from his hospital bed: "We must not let our enemies interfere with our God-given right to victory!"

Interlude in the Cathedral

The Plaza

It's cool and quiet in the cathedral, reverberating with the prayers of the devoted: *viejitas* in mantillas and disintegrating veils; a shriveled man the exact shade of his beige suit; a quartet of nuns from the countryside looking like trussed-up guinea hens. The cathedral may be the only place left in the tropical capital where the lady matador can enjoy a modicum of privacy. From her hip pocket, she takes out the opalescent rosary she just bought on the crumbling cathedral steps.

Above her, stained glass windows depict crusades, the beheadings of holy men, a peculiarly ethereal likeness of the Archangel Gabriel. Sculpted figures of martyrs, many chipped or missing a limb, are set equidistantly along the stone walls. The majority of bullfighters pray to La Virgen Macarena, their patron saint, to keep them safe. But if Suki is partial to any saint, it's to the lank and handsome Sebastian. Unfortunately, there's no altar dedicated to him anywhere here.

A low keening wells up from the front pew, near the empty pulpit. The lady matador recognizes one of the waitresses from the Hotel Miraflor. A wall of color seems to surround her, an eerie, impenetrable blue. Her hands are clasped at her throat in a gesture of grief. Suki stands still for a moment, as though waiting for the *paso doble* to signal the start of a fight. Suddenly, she feels awkward—too tall, her gold slippers clownish. This isn't where she needs to be. Suki retreats to the alcove of the Virgin Mary, with its terrace of flames, to light fourteen candles to her mother.

The poet enters the cathedral with trepidation. He's followed the lady matador here, uncertain of what he'll do. He wants to compare their near-death experiences, write her an epic, seduce her inch by inch. It's been years since he's set foot in a church, not because it was forbidden in Cuba but because he's mistrustful of religion. His mother, once devout, swore by the healing powers of worship. Ricardo could argue credibly in favor of serendipity, magic, the unpredictable crosscurrents of fate. But if he believes anything, it's that faith has no meaning in the modern world.

Ricardo breathes in the stale cathedral air, redolent with incense, and feels his neck muscles tensing up. An inexplicable urge to drink tamarind juice from a chalice heightens his anxiety. The ceiling peels with frescoes of cherubs, plump and frolicking in the once-fluffy clouds. Not a single one is brown-skinned, like his baby Isabel. If it were up to the church, the whole world would be white. On the altar, gleaming like a secret passageway to another kingdom, is a golden tabernacle. Vases of red gladiolas guard it on both sides.

The poet notices the pretty waitress from the garden restaurant, kneeling up front. She's wearing a long, woven blouse the color of egg yolks. Cautiously, he approaches her, as if she were a wounded animal. His footfalls grow louder against the tombstone floors. Nearby, white petals float in a baptismal font.

The waitress catches his eye and they stand transfixed by one another. Then she motions for the poet to follow her. Ricardo is puzzled but does as she requests. She leads him to a confessional on the far side of the cathedral, urging him past the faded damask curtain into the priest's paneled vestibule. A cobweb dangles in a corner next to a mound of dark sawdust left by woodworms. Ricardo tastes the vinegary breath of dispensed contrition, the musty folds of old priests' robes. The sliding meshed window is open for penitents, its hasps fixed by rust.

"My name is Aura," the waitress begins. "I have something to confess."

"I'm sorry, but you must be—"

"What I'm planning to do can't be consoled," she interrupts.

"Listen to me, I'm not—" Ricardo tries again, dry-mouthed. He has no role to play here, no expiation or answers to offer. If she wants to self-flagellate, she doesn't need him.

"I'm going to kill a man. Do you understand?"

The afternoon mass is under way. Ricardo imagines prayers uncoiling around him like streamers. So many countless intentions turned to ash. A bony man trudges along the Stations of the Cross, asthmatically whining promises, weeping into dirty-fisted hands. Ricardo listens to Aura's ragged breathing: two long breaths followed by three fast ones, like the *clave*. This is the second confession he's heard in three days. First, that Korean in the broken elevator. And now this. Everyone must think he has the potato face of a goddamn priest.

"Few things can be looked at in just one way," Ricardo says with as much empathy as he can muster. From the corner of his eye, he spots Suki lighting candles in an alcove for the Virgin Mary. Aura also sees her and stares.

"People say what the lady matador does is murder," the poet continues tentatively. "But it's also transcendence."

Anything can be rationalized, he thinks. Entire populations of innocents have been rationalized off the planet. Look at the destruction unleashed on his island alone. But evil? That's another force entirely. Ricardo, too, has things to confess. How he needs to strike back at his wife, restore his pride, prove that he can be a good father, no matter his wandering eye. How he desperately wants to make love to the lady matador. How even this might not be enough.

The waitress sounds despondent on the other side of the priest's divide. She clenches and unclenches a fist over her breast. "I can't escape what I have to do."

"You must have a good reason." Ricardo wants to reach out and comfort her but something holds him back.

"He killed my brother. And hundreds more."

"Will killing him save anyone else?" He hears the wood creaking as Aura shifts her weight from one knee to the other. "I'm not sure. Times have changed."

"So why now?" Ricardo asks.

"Because my brother asked me to." Aura's voice breaks.

Ricardo is envious of the waitress's ability to speak with the dead. He hesitates, afraid that his own misplaced longings might interfere with his judgment.

"I don't know what to tell you." Ricardo clears his throat. "But my mother used to say that when the dead speak, you must listen."

The waitress stands, leans a hip against the prayer ledge. *"Gracias,"* she whispers, bowing curtly, then leaves.

CHAPTER SIX

The poet defends himself on a city bus • A plot against the military • The Korean's mistress gives birth • The ex-guerrilla takes revenge • The news

FRIDAY

From everything a little remained.

—Carlos Drummond de Andrade

A City Bus

Isabel is awake and squirming in her father's arms. Every cell in her body, it seems to Ricardo, is programmed to grow, grow, grow. She's gained a pound since he and Sarah arrived with their cans of vitamin-packed formula. The poet scans the other passengers on the bus. He can tell he's an object of mirth here. It's not every day that the locals get to see a foreigner on their route, much less a middle-aged one struggling with an infant and twenty pounds of accoutrements in tow.

Ricardo carried far fewer things when he crossed the Straits of Florida twenty-three years ago. In Cuba nobody had special supplies for their children, except milk coupons when times were good. People padded sinks with blankets for cribs, made toys out of twigs and sticks. His daughter grew up with only the barest necessities. An appointment with a top pediatrician, like the one he has today, would've been an inconceivable luxury.

"Is she yours?" the rotund woman next to him asks.

"I'm adopting her." He's relieved, at least, that Isabel isn't giving off an "I'm being kidnapped" air. "We're going to the doctor's."

"How much did you pay for her?" This question, less gentle, comes from an ill-dressed man across the aisle. He's short and sinewy and looks like he could throw a good punch.

"Only the mother's expenses," Ricardo lies. He's heard about the controversy over international adoptions and doesn't want to get caught in the cross fire. He tries to open his window but it's stuck.

"Are you the grandfather?" someone else questions him.

"No, the father." How odd he must look: a fifty-two-year-old man, no longer svelte, adopting this dark-skinned girl from the tropics. Ricardo stares straight ahead, hoping to avoid further questions. A gray gust of exhaust envelops the bus, making him cough. The wound in his chest throbs. He thinks about the waitress in the cathedral. Did she kill a man today? Did he imagine the whole thing?

Ricardo feels the heat of the other passengers' disapproving stares. He knows he'd appear less suspicious if his wife were with him but Sarah had to catch a plane back to New York this morning. Her father had suffered a stroke and was taken to Lenox Hill Hospital. Their adoption lawyer, that gorgon of a woman, demanded that Ricardo return Isabel to her custody. By some miracle, he managed to convince her that his wife would be back by Sunday and that he should keep Isabel for continuity's sake.

"Are you going to raise her yourself or sell her to a hospital?" The ill-dressed man starts in again, raising his voice so that everyone can hear him.

"I have no idea what you're talking about."

"Why were you at the hospital?" He points to the medical bracelet on the poet's wrist.

"I was stabbed in an alley, if you must know," Ricardo lashes out. "I barely escaped with my life!"

He wants to tell everyone how he was forced to study Russian in high school, too, but they'd probably find that irrelevant. Or that he was unfairly imprisoned on the Isle of Pines as an "undesirable." Ricardo wasn't nearly as radical as the other inmates there: not a flaming queer, not prone to suicide or setting fires; merely fond of verse and his waist-length ponytail. For this he spent eleven months in jail.

"What were you doing that someone stabbed you?" the bus driver shouts from the front. Who the hell asked his opinion?

"Yes, what?" clucks a double-chinned woman.

"My sister says Israeli tourists bought her neighbor's boy, then had his body carved up for his kidneys and heart." This is from a young mother with a trio of brats.

"That's unspeakable," Ricardo mumbles.

"What did you say?" the ill-dressed man demands.

"I said people like that deserve the same fate." Ricardo has had enough. If he stays on this bus any longer, there's apt to be a fistfight. He gathers Isabel and all her paraphernalia and gets off at the next stop.

There's a copse of eucalyptus trees and a sorry-looking golf course a hundred yards off. A plaque on a nearby gate reads MINERVA PARK. One of the republic's first presidents was entranced by Minerva, the Roman goddess of wisdom. The president built Greek-style temples in her honor and vowed to turn the country into the Athens of the New World. All the while, he looted the treasury, neglected schools, built up the armed forces, and invited the Universal Fruit Company to ravage his country.

In the pediatrician's waiting room, Ricardo busies himself with magazines, avoiding eye contact with the other mothers. Nobody trusts a man alone with a baby. There's not a thing he can do, it seems, to prove his worthiness as a father. Over the years, Estrella refused to send him photos of Barbarita or acknowledge his paternity in any meaningful way. All she was interested in was the cash he could send.

"She has a slight arrhythmia," Dr. Emilio Zauch says, listening to Isabel's heart. His potbelly swivels toward Ricardo as he speaks. "Nothing to be terribly concerned about but please mention this to her future physician. Extra care is in order before administering anesthesia."

Late that night, the poet walks along the hotel corridors, pushing a sleeping Isabel in her stroller. He starts on the top floor and works his way to the bottom, then back up again. One of the stroller's front wheels is squeaking but Isabel is oblivious to everything. It will take years before she understands the significance of what happened today. Ricardo imagines families around the capital tucked in for the night. Mothers and fathers and children bundled up and snug in their certainty of one another.

Sarah called tonight to say that her father had died and that she wanted a divorce, as if these two events were inextricably linked. Sarah said that her lawyer sister would take care of the details. His wife emphasized that she wanted to *keep the baby* but *get rid of* him. Those were her exact words. Ricardo tried every combination of phrases he could think of to dissuade her, but nothing worked. Worse still, Sarah called Frau Stüber and told her everything. Now he's supposed to return Isabel in the morning. Even from afar, his wife is still calling the shots. He already lost one daughter in Cuba, Ricardo thinks bitterly. He refuses to lose another.

The poet takes the elevator to the ninth floor and returns to their room. He hasn't seen a soul for hours. The empty king-sized bed stares back at him, all starched attention. Ricardo regrets that he and Sarah hadn't made love in months. Perhaps it's his fault that she's leaving him. The truth is that if he'd had the courage, he would've left her first. Their last time together, Sarah got tired of sucking his *pinga* and told him to finish himself off. Then she rolled over and fell asleep. It didn't help that he'd had a bad merengue playing in his head. Lately, sex took a lot longer for him and Sarah had zero patience. When he was a young man, he'd had to hold himself back or risk his first wife's wrath.

Ricardo parks the stroller next to the armchair by the window, opens the curtains, and settles down to ruminate. The palm trees are dimly visible in the darkness, rustling their inquietudes. Long ago, he'd read in a medieval almanac that virgins always knew when a tree was ailing. If he were a mystic, he might see meaning in every detail—the motionless spider on the bedside lamp; the moon shrouded by torn-up clouds. A plethora of mindless clues.

Most of his wife's clothes are folded neatly in the dresser. Ricardo rummages through her belongings and finds the familiar cotton nightgowns she wore to bed every night. Sarah likes to dress in white, in the kitchen and out. Sometimes he'd offered her a touch of color, a carnation for her hair, or an old-fashioned corsage like the kind his mother wore to weddings in Cuba. But Sarah insisted on white. Tucked in among her things is a black-and-red garter belt. Ricardo fingers the hooks and delicate lace, the tiny satin rose at the waist. Had she been planning to wear this for him? It pains him to think that she was hoping to reignite their love life.

Across the courtyard, a light comes on two floors below, spectrally illuminating a balcony. Only time is predictable now, Ricardo thinks, the assurance of one hour following the next. Everything else hangs by a worn blue thread. The poet packs his wife's things into a suitcase, then unpacks them again. He tries to reassure himself. Until the adoption goes through, anything can happen. Ricardo lifts Isabel from her stroller, presses his cheek to hers. This time, he won't let his daughter go.

Room 1017

Hijos de puta. The colonel is disgusted but not surprised. His spies unearthed the information, and it's solid, corroborated. The insurgents are right under his nose at the Hotel Miraflor. The head bartender, the one who makes those killer *mojitos* (a Cuban drink, no less), the one who taught that damn parrot to spout revolutionary gibberish, has turned out to be the mastermind behind the explosions in the capital. The biggest blast, the colonel has learned, is scheduled for the closing banquet of the military conference tomorrow night.

It could take a hundred armed men to do what is necessary. Martín buzzes for his attaché, an ambitious young captain named Trujillo, who appears at his office in seven seconds, impeccable as ever. He's built small and lean for a soldier but he's 99 percent killing machine. Trujillo's greatest regret is that he was too young to fight during the worst years of the civil war.

"Sir?" Trujillo salutes the colonel.

"We've got work to do."

"Ready for orders, sir."

"I want these sons of bitches rounded up by dawn." Martín hands him a list of forty-two subversives, starting with that fucking parrot-loving bartender. "We need the police station basement reopened, a stack of blindfolds delivered. We're going to have ourselves a party."

"Yes, sir." Trujillo tries to suppress a grin.

"Have the warden put together a firing squad by tomorrow midnight. We'll know everything we need to know by then."

"And the disposal of the bodies, sir?"

"I'll see to that. Now get a move on. We don't have much time."

The captain salutes him again.

"Trujillo?"

"Sir?"

"The past is not yet dead."

"Yes, sir!"

Those leftists were fools to think they could escape him, Martín thinks. He'll relish witnessing their terror, inscribing refined sufferings on their skin. In the depths of the police station basement, only the dead will dare smile. What the informers couldn't tell him was who his assailants were en route to the bullring. If they hadn't shot up that taxi driver, Martín might've imagined the entire wretched incident.

Now more than ever, he sees assassins everywhere, sharpshooters aiming their rifles at him. They follow him to the toilet, stalk him in his sleep. Martín reaches for the bottle of antacid he keeps in his desk drawer, takes a chalky-tasting swig. On any given day, his enemies would love nothing more than to see him six feet underground. He takes pride in this fact. Why, he'd sooner die in a hail of bullets than from fucking gout. A Yankee sergeant told him once that only his equal or better could kill him. *Bueno*, there aren't too many of them around.

It's well after midnight when Martín walks from headquarters back to the hotel. It's the last thing his enemies would expect him to do. The trees look bare and ominous in the fog, judging him under their branches. The moon mocks him with its missing sliver, as though he himself were not whole. Or maybe it's his growling stomach working its distortions. No matter, he's sick of playing it safe. Martín stops at an all-night food stand and orders two pork tacos, extra spicy. When he tries to pay, the vendor nervously tells him they're on the house. *Y por la gloria de la patria*, he adds for good measure. The tacos are juicy and delicious and Martín eats them in four bites.

The colonel crosses the street behind the cathedral, ignoring the traffic lights. The sidewalk is buckled under the portals and garbage lines the gutters. An old-fashioned barber's post gleams on the corner, teeming with insects bewitched by the light. The homeless are bedding down where they can for the night. It's impossible for the rich to avoid the poor here, no matter their layers of expensive safety precautions. What respect he gets, Martín knows, is due entirely to his uniform. Without it, he'd be just another dirty *indio* with graying hair.

The hotel guards raise their machine guns but Martín waves them off. It's impossible to tell who's who in this fog. The guards are terrified by their mistake but the colonel is in no mood to let them off the hook by indulging their apologies. Martín pushes his way through the revolving doors. His droopy eye flickers with fatigue. If he goes straight to bed, he might get a couple of hours' sleep. He'll need to be alert for tomorrow. The rounded-up prisoners will be waiting for him at dawn.

The colonel looks both ways before heading down the plushly carpeted hallway to his room. On his floor a tall, disheveled man passes by, pushing a baby stroller. He reaches for his pistol but the weary father pays him no mind. Martín remembers the long nights with his own Antonio, his raw, colicky face. That seems a century ago.

His door is double bolted, as he left it, with the DO NOT DIS-TURB sign in place. The bathroom light is on, also as he left it. The colonel takes a quick piss, chews a handful of antacid pills, and collapses into bed wearing only his boxer shorts. He leaves his pistol on the nightstand and sets the alarm for five o'clock.

Martín arranges the pillows around his head, tucking the blanket in at his waist. If he gets overly hot, he'll dream of the river ghost again. The same nightmare has been plaguing him. Last night, it beckoned to him from a far, frozen shore. In the dream, Martín is a boy of eight or nine, anxiously searching the cats in town (they've multiplied to thousands) for the one who'll turn into La Viciosa. "Is it you?" he interrogates each cat, as the nearby river crackles with ice. Each time Martín has this dream, he wakes up in a sweat, afraid he might already be dead.

A tremor of light filters in through a break in the curtains, from the still-mocking moon. Martín closes his eyes and tries to relax, concentrating on one muscle group at a time: face, neck, buttocks, legs. He can hear the rush of his pulse in his ears. He doesn't want to sleep alone, not tonight. Insomnia isn't an option but he's run out of sleeping pills, and it's too late to call for a whore. Thoughts of the lady matador fill his head. Martín pictures her in the basement of the police station, stripped naked and begging for her life. Yes, that's how he'd like her, he thinks, rubbing his cock. It doesn't take long to make himself come and fall deeply asleep.

The Factory

When he started smoking cigarettes at fourteen, Won Kim was much better at blowing smoke rings: perfect blue-gray ovals that rose to his bedroom ceiling before breaking up into wispy constellations. Now the best he can manage are wobbly semicircles that drift aimlessly overhead. He has half a mind to suck them back into his lungs, incubate them until they turn into toxic brown spots. Given a choice, he would ingest all his mistakes this way.

It has been a long day at the factory. A half hour before closing, Won Kim gave his employees Saturday off with full pay. The troublemaker offered him a small pumpkin in gratitude. He knows he is getting too soft with them. It is only a matter of time before he is hit with a backlash of demands and a breakdown in discipline. Nobody trusts leniency in this country. Kindness in a boss is a sign of weakness. Only *caudillos* rule with any respect or longevity.

Won Kim lights another cigarette and unlocks his private file cabinet, where he keeps a bottle of *soju*. He pours himself a glass, revisiting the problems that orbit him ceaselessly: he is too inept and cowardly to kill himself; his mother is dead; his mistress, mercurial as ever, turns sixteen today; he owes thousands of dollars on their honeymoon suite; Glorious Textiles has lost more money this year than it has made in the last three; his reputation is in shambles; he has not gone butterfly hunting in a year (this should probably top his list).

The *soju* burns his throat and spreads through his chest. Won Kim rolls his shoulders to relieve the tension that keeps them hunched. The view outside his window is diminishing with winter: fewer birds, longer shadows, less foliage. He spots a colony of beetles flipping over in a pile of leaves. How he wishes he could spend his life recording these minute dramas of nature.

Once, he had wanted to write the definitive tome on the stages of a butterfly's lifecycle—egg, larva, chrysalis, imago—in the sonorous language of lepidopterology. He might have likened these stages to the evolution of man, or to the making of history, or to romantic love (which, by its nature, is invariably doomed), but he never wrote more than a few dyspeptic sentences. He had fantasized, too, about seducing the perfect woman with his brilliance but neither his brilliance nor the woman ever materialized.

After a second glass of *soju*, Won Kim begins to unwind. He does not get obnoxious the way his compatriots do when they have had too much to drink. Instead he is enveloped in the faded memories he avoids when sober. His first time at his family's summer house in Mallipo, the waves terrified him until his sisters told him that waves were how the ocean rocked itself to sleep. Won Kim soon grew fixated by the sea's daily offerings: marine skeletons, driftwood, the silvery smell of low tides and scampering crabs. Now and then a dead fish would float ashore and he would stare at its boiled-looking eyes and wonder what had killed it.

Won Kim drinks a third glass of *soju* and rests his head on his desk. Nothing scares him more than the ocean and its unpredictable jellyfish. During those vacations in Mallipo, his father would take an invigorating swim every day. He'd swim out as far as the horizon, or so it seemed to Won Kim, until he wondered whether his father would ever return. (At times, he hoped his father had drowned but he'd soon be stricken with remorse.) To this day, Won Kim prefers the woods and the mountains, the safety of oxygen. As his father grew old and sickened, his face fell to bone but his voice never wavered. Whatever will fall has already fallen, Won Kim tells himself.

Won Kim blinks and looks around him. The darkness feels three-dimensional. Only the green light on his computer blinks back. Several hours have passed. His mouth is parched, his neck and shoulders sore from sleeping doubled over on his desk. He turns on the office television to catch the headline news. Hurricane Odette has bypassed Central America altogether, hitting a stretch of Texas instead. The injured lady matador will compete in

Sunday's bullfight. The ex-dictator is recovering at Todos Santos Hospital with a couple of bullets in his chest. His popularity has shot up 6 percent. Each day, Won Kim thinks, is an inexplicable wilderness.

He grabs his briefcase and locks the factory doors on his way out. The bats stir in the sapodilla trees. At least his car is where he left it. Two previous ones were stolen from this very spot. Won Kim reaches into the glove compartment for the boxes of caramels he keeps hidden there. They are made in Japan, delicious and guilt-inducing at once. His father had lived through the miseries of World War II and taught his children to hate everything Japanese. When he finally opened an office in Tokyo, he cheated his enemies at every turn.

Traffic is unexpectedly heavy into the city. A screech-owl rises up from a gnarled pine by the roadside. The radio blasts a Christian sermon with standard threats about the fiery hereafter. Won Kim leaves the program on for satirical effect. After twelve sweltering summers in the tropics, he is certainly not afraid of hell.

As he nears the cathedral, a spectral woman circles the plaza with a battered bucket of what appears to be blood. Occasionally, she stops to dip her feet in the viscous liquid. Then she continues her procession, leaving a spiral of footprints. Nobody but him seems to notice her. Won Kim wonders whether the woman is an apparition, sent to him as a message from the dead.

Security is tight at the hotel. The word on the street is that another bomb will go off in the city tonight. But if he paid attention to every rumor, he would never get out of bed. Won Kim surrenders his car to the valets. He considers stopping at the fortune-teller's kiosk in the shopping arcade. She is open most evenings and is said to employ human divining bones to impressive effect. Won Kim has seen her strolling through the lobby, wobbly on tumescent ankles, wearing long gypsy skirts and crystal necklaces. On an impulse, he goes to the florist shop, which is also open late. The salesclerk, petite and fox-faced, helps him arrange a birthday bouquet for his mistress. Most of the flowers are hothouse grown—tulips and roses, an impressive array of lilies.

From inside the shop, Won Kim spies the obnoxious Cuban poet trudging by, pushing a baby stroller. Won Kim ducks behind a pillar and watches him. An ostentatious bandage bulges from under his guayabera. Won Kim bristles with resentment. Everyone, it seems, has managed to hurt themselves except for him. He looks both ways before racing over to the elevators, and is relieved when the first one is empty. The hallway on his floor is empty, too, and he detects a faint scent of burnt sugar. He feels a sudden, curious sting in his nipples.

In the honeymoon suite, the curtains are drawn and his mistress is in bed, propped up with mounds of embroidered pillows. She is wearing a loose, lacy nightgown with cerulean ribbons on the collar. On the beveled edge of the nightstand is a glass of pure white milk. Berta looks at him tenderly from across the unlit room. She is humming a discordant melody that he dimly recognizes, a nocturnal bird's song. The faint notes seem to him a precious substance. At her side, wrapped snugly in one of his flying-elephants blankets, is a baby, sound asleep.

Won Kim approaches them, hesitantly, and sees the fat-cheeked boy, a glossy replica of him: the same bulging eyes and wedge of nose, the same round, bald, fragile skull. It is like coming upon a lost part of himself.

Won Kim lays the birthday bouquet at the foot of their bed— for Berta, for his son. He wants to say something but cannot find the words. The moment is too sublime. He begins to stammer until his mistress holds a finger to her lips.

"I named him after you," she whispers. "I named him Won Kim."

Room 1017

The ex-guerrilla walks past a fancy cutlery store downtown. In the window is a hologram of a woman throwing a fork at a man's throat, presumably her husband's. Aura doesn't see the slightest humor in this. It's her day off but she's too restless to wait at home. A sticky muck on the street tugs at her shoes. She steps inside the Tres Leches bakery, drawn by the fresh bread scent. Aura picks up a plastic tray and tongs, selects a sugar bun and a piece of pineapple cake, and brings them to the cashier to tally up. She eats her pastries with a *café con leche,* while standing at the counter.

A movie theater down the street is garishly lit up with colored bulbs. A 1950s Mexican film festival is under way and Aura decides to go. A sleepy clerk takes her money, then follows Aura into the dim lobby. She buys a box of candy devils from the moldering display, then drifts into the middle of a movie she's never heard of—*Víctimas del pecado.* It takes a moment for her eyes to adjust. The screen looks smoky to her, a scrim of ash. The moth-eaten curtains hang listlessly to one side. The walls are red, as is the nappy carpet. She suspects that in its off-hours, the theater shows pornography.

Aura looks around and sees a couple kissing passionately in the back row. They're the only other people in the theater. Aura samples the devil candy, with its spicy cinnamon flavor. It's a relief to be tucked away where no one can find her. She settles back to watch the film. It's about a gorgeous cabaret singer, Violeta, who rescues an abandoned infant from a garbage dump and raises him as her own. It's clichéd and incredibly corny but Aura is mesmerized, especially by the musical numbers. The Cuban mambo king Pérez Prado is in it. The fluidity of his movements reminds her a little of the colonel.

When the movie is over, Aura doesn't get up immediately. She wants to sit in the theater for a while and become someone else; the lady matador, perhaps—or better yet, a zephyr, a zero, pure air. Anything or anyone except who she needs to be.

It's late when she finally leaves the theater. The silvery leaves of the eucalyptus trees spangle like tinsel. A clanking truck's fumes overwhelm her. There's a taxi idling on the corner with a brown-robed saint on its dashboard: Saint Francis of Assisi. The hotel is only four blocks away but Aura can't force herself to take another step. She gets in the cab and asks the driver to cruise around the city for ten or fifteen minutes. He speeds down a maze of one-way streets, running up the meter. Aura doesn't object. She wants to ride in the cab all night, stay enveloped in its dependable tobacco smell. The radio is playing a sad song, possibly in Arabic. She'd gladly listen to it for hours.

Aura looks out the taxi window and tries not to watch the homeless families and drunks, the trickle of pedestrians with their grinding solitudes; a haggard *guarumo* tree, blackened from soot. Instead she angles her gaze upward, toward the down-trodden grandeur of the buildings, to the chipped lintels and cherubs, gargoyles and rococo cornices, reminders of the city's colonial past. She passes the cathedral, its spires looking slightly askew, and thinks of the lady matador's treasure of candles burning inside, of the hapless poet who tried to give her advice.

Above her a quarter-moon floats in the sky, threshing stars.

It's the hour of no hour. Anyone awake is either an insomniac or up to no good. Aura understands what she must do, cleanly and without fuss. The luxury of debate is over. After all, her brother didn't get a chance to decide his fate. Murder isn't so arduous when the victim is unsuspecting. In the heat of the moment, even the guilty don't really believe they'll die. Aura knows that the colonel is suspicious by nature. Didn't he interrogate her when she delivered his arsenic-laced coffee? And he knew enough not to touch a drop. Sedatives would make her job easier—both for him and for her. She should've thought of this before.

Aura is waiting in the cedar-lined closet of the colonel's hotel room. She's safe in the closet because the colonel prefers storing his belongings, few but precious, in the chest of drawers: a silver flask; cuff links with a Mayan design; a pocket-sized photo album of two half-grown boys, probably his children, though they look nothing like him. They, too, will be her victims, these boys.

The colonel has been asleep for over an hour. His snoring is steady and strong. Fortunately, Aura didn't have to wait long for him to fall asleep once he returned to his room. A visit to the bathroom, some fussing and rearranging of pillows, and he was out. At least he didn't turn on the television. Men like him always hope to hear flattering news of themselves.

Aura is tempted to kill the colonel with his own pistol, make the world think he took his life. This is the ultimate humiliation for a military man. Instead she brought a knife, the sharpest in the hotel kitchen. She removes it now from her satchel. It's eight inches long and slightly curved, used for butchering beef and lamb. But the colonel isn't a lamb. He's a killer of children, of brothers and lovers, a destroyer of lives. His life is nothing on balance with thousands of others. If there were an orderly way to set him on fire, Aura would do it. For symmetry's sake.

The curtains are drawn but the moon's faint light slips between the panels, projecting a delicate embroidery on his bed. Her own shadow looms behind her, the spike of knife dark in her hand. With any luck, the colonel will die not knowing what killed him. Aura approaches his bed, her breath inaudible (another trick she learned in the jungle). She must stop her hand from trembling, or risk making a mess. Once the enemy is identified, the Cuban pamphlets said, you must act, not think.

The colonel mumbles in his sleep, startling her. One eyelid is quivering and his right forefinger straightens and bends. Aura watches him so intently that she enters his dream. There's a boy on a frozen riverbank and he's frantically waving a stick to someone offshore. Cats are loitering everywhere, straggling toward the boy on withered, faltering legs. Aura narrows her eyes and sees a hand beckoning from the leaden river, a drowning man or woman, she can't tell which. The boy is crying as he runs from cat to cat, slipping on the ice. Then he stops before her, gazing up at her face.

"Is it you, Viciosa?" he asks. Tears leak from the colonel's eyes. Then he opens them and smiles at Aura in the darkness.

"You're here," he says wistfully.

She presses the knife to his throat. His arms go limp in surrender; one under the covers, the other above. Aura holds his life in her hands like a cold, bright bead.

"I know who you are," he gasps, perplexed.

A smell of urine fills the room. The colonel is puddled in it. Aura doesn't want to feel sorry for him but she can't bear not feeling anything, either. She's tired of the exhausting rounds of wounding, of recycling mournful things. *Act, don't think.*

An uprush of air makes the curtains billow inward. Aura's back stiffens and her arms grow prickly. She pushes the colonel's head back, feels the sharp stubble of his cheek. A ribbon of blood oozes along the edge of the blade. If she doesn't kill him now, he'll kill her. She needs to believe this.

"Close your eyes," she orders and presses hard into the growing flap of skin.

Instead the colonel's eyes widen as the blood drenches his neck and chest. Its mineral scent coats Aura's breath. His tongue protrudes thickly, a small platform of flesh. She debates whether to let him suffer, or extend him the courtesy she'd accord the lowliest dog. Aura grants him this last mercy.

The cathedral bells toll the hour: once, twice, three times, four. She imagines smoke rising from the colonel's dead hide, fleeing his bones for good; turkey vultures hunched and waiting in the branches of trees. Aura studies the colonel's face, feels trapped by it, as if in a magnificent empty mirror. The last word in history, she fears, must be fought for again and again.

The News

From *Lo Último*

Animal rights activists broke into the municipal bullring today, setting loose two of the beasts to be used in Sunday's highly anticipated Battle of the Lady Matadors. Several activists were injured when one of the bulls charged them into the bleachers. The other bull managed to escape the ring and lunged its way through the nearby flower market, upsetting vendors' carts and destroying a cell phone kiosk. Police officers finally cornered the beast and shot it dead.

"It's an outrage," fumed Pilar García, leader of Bulls for Humanity. "Bullfighting is nothing more than sadism, pure and simple!" García prostrated herself in the middle of the bullring before being forcibly removed by police. Promoter Guillermo Cabeza Dura contested her accusations. "This is legitimate art!" he shouted at reporters as the defiant García was dragged off. He vowed that the Battle of the Lady Matadors would proceed as planned. "I won't let a bunch of leaf eaters interfere with the glories of an illustrious tradition!"

From Radio Evangélica

Radio Evangélica: We're here at Todos Santos Hospital at the bedside of our republic's next president. The general was brought here after the latest cowardly attack on his life. How are you feeling today, General?

General: Get rid of those fucking flowers! It looks like a goddamn funeral parlor in here—

R.E.: We're on the air, General. I'm sure our listeners want to hear how you're doing and—

H.G.: Jesus Christ! Turn that thing off!!

[*Sounds of scuffling and more cursing*]

If you don't get the hell out, I'll kill you with my bare hands!

R.E. (*In a strangled voice*): Perhaps we can return at a more convenient time then. Up next: our *cumbia* versions of Christian favorites. And now, a word from our sponsor.

Voice-over: We know you've worked hard at keeping your soul spotless. But what about your kitchen? We at STAIN-AWAY want to keep every part of your life squeaky clean . . .

From *Hora de Noticias*

Congress passed a law today temporarily freezing international adoptions. Pressure from human rights groups abroad has put lawmakers on the defensive. "Until we can codify the rules governing foreign adoptions," said Senator Silvestre Jiménez, "we must stop all adoptions. Our reputation as a humane society depends on it." Women's groups championed the move. Eugenia Pinchón, president of POW (Protect Our Wombs), was in a triumphant mood outside the capitol and led a parade of supporters, shouting: *"¡Que viva el útero!"*

From *The Lupe Galeano Show*

Lupe Galeano: I'm delighted to have with us here five of the bravest, loveliest lady toreadors in the Western Hemisphere.

We've persuaded these fearsome felines to walk the runway in fashions designed by our very own, incomparably chic Emilio Luz y Luz. As you know, his sensational collections have graced the runways of Paris, Milan, and *Nueva York*. Ladies and gentlemen, please give a warm welcome to Emilio Luz y Luz!

[*Warm applause*]

Emilio Luz y Luz: Thank you, Lupe, a thousand times thank you!

L.G.: Well, you're certainly looking beguiling, Emilio. Are white silk jumpsuits going to be all the rage this winter?

E.L.L.: This is just a preview from my men's spring collection, darling! But ladies first . . . *¿no es cierto*, Lupe?

L.G.: *Pero claro, mi amor*. Now Emilio, are you ready to tell us about these dazzling *matadoras* in your transcendent outfits?

[*Music to* Last Days of Disco *blares from loudspeakers*]

E.L.L.: *Sí, sí, sí!* Up first is the incomparable Lety Betancourt from Venezuela. In her last fight in Caracas, Lety was awarded the ears, tail, and testicles of two ferocious bulls. You look marvelous, *querida*! This feathered frock has been hand-sewn on exquisite Hong Kong silk with 1,137 genuine free-range ostrich feathers. There's no hiding in this sexy number, ladies. In fact, you'll turn so many heads you may just have to recover—on a red velvet divan!

L.G.: Oooooh, I'd like to try that!

[*Audience laughter*]

E.L.L.: And here are our visiting twin *matadoras* from Colombia . . . Laura and Trinidad de Morales! These beauties are known for their intricate moves in the ring. Former ballerinas with the Medellín Ballet Company, they are a vision of grace in what I call my Two-for-One Collection—perfect for sisters, as you can see, or best friends, or even mothers and daughters. See how the bold geometric patterns work separately or—stand together, girls!—juxtapose into a perfect abstract painting . . .

Special Bulletin from *El Pajarito*

Don't forget, today is the most auspicious day of the year to serve pumpkin. Prepare it for everyone you know: your children, your servants, even your domestic pets. It will protect them from the evil that looms over our country like a rain cloud. And remember: You must first be a caterpillar before you can soar like a butterfly! That's all for now, my lovelies.

Epilogue

SUNDAY

The Border

The ex-guerrilla is on a bus heading north. She's in disguise, her head shaven, a stretchy bandage wrapped around her chest. It's itchy and tight and makes her breasts ache. Ghostly cacti rise up in the distance, reflecting the moon's meager light. No one in their right mind would be traveling at this hour, across this inhospitable land, if they weren't desperate. Aura thinks of her sisters back in the capital, praying to their merciless God; how they'd offered her shelter, the respite of immutable days.

The rattling of the bus jangles her nerves. Aura is worn out but too anxious to sleep. She hasn't heard from her brother since before the colonel's murder, not even to praise her for a job well done. There are others on the bus with her, all asleep except for the Cuban poet with the swaddled infant two rows back. He got on the bus early, pretending not to recognize her. He'd shaved off his goatee and seemed jittery. He hasn't stopped whispering either—to himself, or the baby, she isn't sure which. Aura strains to make out his words. She suspects he's reciting verse, overhears the phrase: *the lime tree's agitated shade.* He must be a fugitive, like her.

At the start of the trip, Aura paid the bus driver seven hundred U.S. dollars to get her to Mexico without incident. He swore he knew every border guard personally, that for another five hundred he could arrange a transit visa. The driver turns up the radio to hear the news. A bomb has exploded in the Hotel Miraflor, destroying the ballroom. Two Argentine generals were killed along with a half dozen other military men. Somehow Miguel and his cohorts managed this since yesterday. The colonel's murder is being linked to the bombing. So far the government is blaming the left, which means they don't know anything yet.

Aura looks out her window for a sign of her brother but sees only a caterpillar inching its way along the worm-eaten frame. It looks to her like a pale, severed finger. She pictures an encampment of spirits murmuring in the desert, negotiating in the afterlife what they couldn't settle alive. The ex-guerrilla closes her eyes. She remembers her father listening to birdsong. *That's what they're here for,* hija. *To echo the Lord's joy.* And the nights he showed her, with a sweep of his arm, the skies generous with stars. If only she could keep her eyes closed forever, lift the siege on her heart. She'd be willing to go to her grave for a single evening's peace.

Death glides in on white beautiful wings.

"Goddamn it, Julio. Where've you been?" Aura tries not to move her lips. She looks around but sees no evidence of her brother.

Watching over you.

"How am I supposed to live?"

With joy, far away.

"Where?"

You'll know when the time comes.

"Show me your face. Please."

It's impossible.

"I'm going crazy."

No one can harm you now.

"But I'm lost. And I can't go home."

Aura feels the damp warmth of her brother's breath on her cheek. He seems to be everywhere and nowhere at once.

You can be lost two steps from home.

"This is no time for riddles, Julio. I'm scared and sick to my bones!"

Your work is done. You must find peace.

"But how—"

Te quiero mucho. Adios, hermana . . .

From Channel 9's *Top of the News*

A nationwide manhunt is under way for the killer of Colonel Martín Abel, who was murdered in his room at the Hotel Miraflor hours before a bomb ripped through its grand ball-room. The bomb killed eight high-ranking military officers from around the Americas, all attending a hemispheric conference in the capital. No suspects have been named but investigators suspect leftist terrorists are responsible for the blast. Colonel Abel, a controversial figure during the civil war, is survived by his estranged wife and two young sons . . .

The Airport

Won Kim sits in the international lounge of the airport with his mistress and their infant son, waiting for the late morning flight to Seoul. If his mother were alive, he would not be returning to Korea today. Everything, thankfully, is changed. Now he needs only to care for his family, exhibit kindness and generosity to his sisters (this will not be difficult), carry on with his father's textiles business, or not. Even the gnawing necessity for death seems to have receded like a tide.

Soon Won Kim will inherit a great deal of money. After completing the funeral arrangements for his mother, he will be free to do as he wishes. This is a luxury he could not afford before. His life of transience, of living outside his skin is over. Twelve years ago he had arrived at this very airport. The September heat was searing and the country was in the last throes of civil war. His first week on the job, Won Kim found the mutilated body of a woman in the brush behind his factory. He should have left then, vanished where no one could find him. Instead he continued to work for his father, long after he was dead.

"I'm thirsty," Berta says.

Won Kim buys her a bottle of guava juice and a packet of cashews at the sundries shop. He picks up a newspaper and is gratified to see just one story about him relegated to a back page. Perhaps he will choose to abandon the tropics entirely. He could sell Glorious Textiles to his competitors, or permit the workers to form a cooperative. It amuses Won Kim to think of the headlines: KOREAN MANUFACTURER INCITES LOCAL SOCIALIST EXPERIMENT!

Well, it would be too late to deport him then. The bitterest chapter of his life is already closed.

Won Kim returns to his mistress. He peels back his son's blanket and examines him closely. A bit of mucus bubbles up from a tiny nostril. Won Kim wipes it clean with the tip of his finger. The boy wakes up and puckers his lips. Berta loosens her blouse and, gently, as though she has been doing it all her life, puts him to her breast. As he suckles, the baby waves his dimpled hand to and fro, a tender branch, beckoning Won Kim to the future. It is enough to swell his heart. Won Kim is eager to show his son his first butterfly. And to introduce him to big American breakfasts—pancakes and scrambled eggs with bacon, fried very crisp.

The passengers line up for the flight to Seoul. Won Kim knows each traveler by name, acknowledges them with a nod. They are curious about his young companion and the baby in her arms but he does not indulge their inquisitiveness. Won Kim booked the flight first-class. It cost a fortune but he will take his firstborn home only once. He helps Berta and the baby settle into their window seat.

The stewardess, a comely woman with a northern accent, takes their drink orders.

"Champagne," Won Kim says, and pats his son's plump cheek.

Won Kim thinks that if he were a butterfly, he might be in the last larval stage. The wing disks are not yet visible to the naked eye, tucked away on the second and third thoracic segments. While dormant, these pre-wings will increase strikingly in size until they succeed in rupturing the chrysalis, sloughing off the past amid a carnival of leaves. Then comes the drama of inflating the wings with blood, their drying in the sun; the brief, terrible vulnerability to predators.

But if it survives, Won Kim knows, it will reach the pinnacle of existence. It will finally, gloriously, fly.

From Radio El Pueblo

The Justice Department has ordered the arrest of international adoption lawyer Gertrudis Stüber today on multiple charges of kidnapping, extortion, obstruction of justice, and manslaughter. This last charge comes after an infant boy she entrusted to an American couple from Tennessee died in their custody. Stüber, who plans to defend herself in court, denies all charges.

In a related story, the adoptive father of one of Stüber's high-priced babies has disappeared from the recently bombed Hotel Miraflor with a four-month-old local girl. The adoptive father, Cuban exile and former prison inmate Ricardo Morán, is believed to be armed and dangerous. Anyone with information about Morán or the missing child is urged to contact authorities immediately.

The Bullring

Suki is the last contestant in the inaugural Battle of the Lady Matadors in the Americas. It's been a long afternoon of killing and derision. Two of the *matadoras* were run off by the bulls. The audience rewarded them with a filthy haze of beer cans and cushions. Only Paloma Gómez deserved to steal the time of the crowd. She was formidable today; her footwork impeccable, her cape a lurid blur. Papi was right. Those boxing lessons have paid off. Suki hates to admit it but maybe Paloma should win the competition today. As she left the ring, honored with her bull's bloody ears and tail and the roar of the crowd, Paloma threw back her head, laughing, then glared at Suki, as if to say: *So there, cabrona. Let's see you top that.*

Now it's Suki's turn. She looks out at the unruly crowd thronging the stands. It seems to her that the whole city is here, hungry for violence—the one language without rules. She could wave a handkerchief and signal her surrender, her return to civilian life. The headlines would blare news of her defeat and the scandal might pursue her for a month or two, but then it would be done with. The past would be hers to brood over privately. Nobody need know who she was, or what she'd aspired to be.

The crowd grows quiet, waiting to see what the lady matador will do. The press has been too favorable, fanned expectations unreasonably high. They've made no concessions for her injury, either, or the stiffness of her gait. Anything short of a triumph will invite their contempt. Overhead, a raven divides the sky. Scorched leaves flutter through the ring. In the hidden glare of the isthmus connecting North America to South, Suki is far from officialdom. Anything can happen here.

"*¡Ándale, hija! ¡Ándale!*" Her father's voice rings out from among the thousands of others. She recognizes his head like a shiny black wreath in the stands. Today, she'll defeat death once and for all, Suki decides.

The lady matador squares her shoulders and faces her bull. It's a giant, a cathedral, barely weakened by the lances and barbs. Her *cuadrilla* warned Suki that a mastodon would be brought to her in this ruined city. A bull from the best breeding ranch in Mexico, murderous as the Miura bulls of Spain. A bull like the one that killed Manolete fifty-six years ago, like the bull that mangled her grandfather's leg. A bull with raw, remorseless horns.

The *banderilleros* look more nervous than Suki has ever seen them. No doubt they sense her wavering, envision death chalking a cross on her cape. Or more likely, it's the crowd willing her to fail because for a woman to fail reinforces tradition. To them Suki is a novelty, a passing phenomenon, like the hurricane that never quite arrived. It doesn't matter how spectacular or perilous her performance. Tomorrow, business will return to the maddening usual, to more changeless seasons.

The beast canters across the ring, raising yellow eddies of dust, its eyes fixed on the lady matador. Its hot breath drifts up through her heels, her knees, the pulsing wound in her ribs. She can't arch her back without radiating more pain. Suki blinks and sees her mother's face like a mask over the bull's.

She shakes off the encroaching memories and focuses on the bull's shadow, a brutal violet drawing near her own. Suki lifts her chin and raises her muleta, offering it, flaring, to the beast. *Arrogance, honor, death.* The bull doesn't waste another moment, charging with a thunderous percussion of hooves, its horns low. It passes dangerously close to her waist, then returns for more—and more again. Suki flinches but she is pleased. It's an intrepid *toro*, and tireless. A real *fiero*. They're well matched, joined inextricably on this November day, in this condemnation of light. Both cannot leave the ring alive.

The lady matador pictures herself divine and naked, approaching annihilation. She taunts the bull closer, smears her thighs with its stink. Its meat and muscle are meant for her. Over and again, she urges the bull to meet its fate. But it refuses to give up. Suki spots its *rubios,* as if painted plain as a target high on the hump of its neck.

"*Mi espada,*" she calls out to her sword boy, and her mouth floods with the familiar mineral saltiness. Soon she must plunge the sword high between the bull's shoulders, past its lethal horns, cleanly sever its vena cava.

Suki removes her *montera* out of respect for the beast. It's a valiant opponent, worthy of notoriety, of immortality. If she succeeds today, nobody present will ever forget that this kingly bull lived and how magnificently it died. Suki will retire her cape and her suit of lights, embrace a quieter banishment. Yes, if she succeeds today, she'll finally take leave of the ring, of her grieving, of her mother. The bull lifts its gargantuan head, gauging the distance between them. Then with a terminal surge of strength, it charges. Suki is talented in this sacrament of killing and she wants, with this last thrust, to make death most eloquent.

Acknowledgments

Mil gracias to my dear friends and readers: Chris Abani, Micheline Aharonian Marcom, Tony Cohan, and Laleh Khadivi. Also, my deepest gratitude to Alexis Gargagliano, my brilliant new editor, who loves nothing more than to make sentences sing, and sing again.

About the Author

Cristina García is the author of five novels, including the National Book Award finalist *Dreaming in Cuban;* children's books; anthologies; and poetry. Her work has been translated into a dozen languages, and she is the recipient of a Guggenheim Fellowship and a Whiting Writers' Award, among other honors. She has taught literature and writing at numerous universities, and divides her time between Texas and northern New Mexico.

31901047546892